To Claim a
WILDE

Kimberly Kaye Terry

⊕ HARLEQUIN® KIMANI™ ROMANCE

Recycling programs
for this product may
not exist in your area.

ISBN-13: 978-0-373-86417-1

To Claim a Wilde

H HARLEQUIN®

™ www.Harlequin.com

Printed in U.S.A.

Kimberly Kaye Terry's love for reading romances began at an early age. To date she's an award-winning author of over twenty novels in romance, paranormal romance and erotic romance, has garnered acclaim for her work and happily calls writing her full-time job. Kimberly has a bachelor's degree in social work and a master's degree in human relations and has held licenses in social work and mental health therapy in the United States and abroad.

She and her daughter volunteer weekly at various social-service agencies, and Kimberly is a long-standing member of Zeta Phi Beta Sorority, Inc., a community-conscious organization. Kimberly is a naturalist and practices aromatherapy. She believes in embracing the powerful woman within each of us and meditates on a regular basis. Kimberly would love to hear from you. Visit her at kimberlykayeterry.com.

Books by Kimberly Kaye Terry

Harlequin Kimani Romance

Visit the Author Profile page at Harlequin.com for more titles.

I have a few dedications, so bear with me.

First, to my amazing kiddo, Hannah. She is, and has always been, an amazing young person. It's my true blessing to see her grow up into such a wonderful young lady. Even when she thinks I'll let her wear my stilettos. Not even… ;) Momma loves you, baby girl!

To my fans. I'm a blessed woman to have some of the BEST, sexiest, funniest, craziest and, most of all, supportive reading divas! You all are, absolutely, the best. After having major surgery, I was knocked off my feet for nearly a year. There were days I wanted to scream as I dealt with recovery, physical therapy and everything that goes along with major surgery. I received so many beautiful emails from you all, emails that often helped me power through the pain and finish this story!! I'm better, and now back to writing full-time again. And so, of course, that means I have *so* many Wildes in my head yelling at me to tell their story, and I plan to write them for you. I love you all!

I'd like to also dedicate this to two people who were patient, understanding and just plain awesome as I went through some hard days recovering, when I just didn't feel like writing. Glenda Howard, my amazing editor, and Ethan Ellenberg, my equally amazing agent. I have no words for how supportive you two were. I do have them, but I don't want to cry and mess up my makeup. A diva has to keep her composure!

Last, but not least, to two women who are more like sisters than friends: Yolanda Turner and Marvenette White. I don't know what I would have done without you two… and you know why. Don't worry…I won't tell, lol!

Chapter 1

"Hey, Canton, check her out, damn. Man…now that's what you call fine as *hell*!"

Canton Wilde barely refrained from wincing at the sound of his friend's booming voice that he could *still* hear over the loud pumping music being blasted by the massive speakers throughout the building.

Ray was a great friend, great employee, great drinking partner and overall great guy…but volume control, especially when he'd been drinking, was definitely not his strength.

Or something easy to ignore.

The fact that Ray was doing his damnedest to find a candidate for Canton for a one-night stand didn't make it any easier to ignore either his friend's loud voice *or* his intentions.

Yet he'd allowed Ray to convince him to come out for "game night" at one of their favorite watering holes.

He glanced toward the woman Ray was obviously talking about, his beer halfway to his mouth, giving her a casual once-over.

The tall, striking blonde was eyeing him as though he was manna from heaven and her last supper.

He ran an assessing glance over the woman, head to toe, as she posed, cue in hand, butt reared out as she leaned over the pool table, readying her shot.

Already tall, she wore red stilettos that matched the barely there body-hugging scarlet dress, which left nothing to the imagination.

The plunging neckline pushed and pressed up a truly mouthwatering set of breasts, Canton thought, in pure masculine appreciation.

Probably fake.

But hell, she wore 'em well, he thought.

As she leaned over the cue, he knew it was all for show; she'd angled herself to give Canton a good long look at what she had to offer. She was poised for maximum effect, showing off her full hips and round behind.

He briefly wondered if her ass was fake, too. With the growing trend it wasn't out of the ordinary. He liked a nice rear end on a woman, just like the next man. But he preferred the real deal. One that was firm, but soft to touch.

She made the shot and flipped Canton a triumphant smile, showing perfect winter-white teeth.

She turned to her pool partner, another female, and gave her a high five for the well-made shot before hopping up on her stool.

She wrapped her long hand with its dagger-length crimson-painted nails around her glass and took a delicate sip of her drink.

Canton's attention, oddly, focused on her long nails, and how perfectly sculpted they were…and how unappealing they were to him.

Something else new for him.

Before, he would have been imagining what those nails could do on his body.

She casually positioned her shapely legs at a perfect angle for Canton to see that she was sans panties. Then flashed him a wink.

If the vibe the blonde was giving off hadn't been an indication of her interest in him, definitely the audacious flash of bare ass and show of her kitty was, as she returned his stare, boldly and equally assessing.

Her full crimson lips turned up in a seductive little grin…a calculated grin, as she held his gaze.

Canton knew immediately that she was down for…*whatever*.

But Canton was not.

As attractive and obviously willing as she was, Canton just wasn't interested.

He gave her a barely discernible nod of acknowledgment for the well-played shot and with a small salute of his beer, brought the bottle to his mouth and turned away.

As he shifted away, Canton noticed her crimson lips turn downward in a soured look of irritation and a hint of embarrassment.

He just wasn't interested. Not in a one-night stand and definitely not with a woman he didn't know, not tonight.

In fact, he hadn't felt the need for that type of adult play in a while. Had it been six months ago, *and* had he been a single man, no doubt about it, it would have been a different scenario playing out.

But a lot had happened in his world over the past six months, things that made a man look at the world in a slightly different way.

"What the..." He turned at Ray's incredulous tone. "Are you serious?" Canton barely refrained from truly laughing out loud at the disbelieving look that crossed his friend's dark brown face. Unknown to him, Ray had been watching the entire exchange.

"Man, you *have got* to be kidding me!" He shook his head, momentarily at a loss for words. "I thought you were a Wilde!"

Canton's eyes narrowed as he swallowed the beer lodged in his throat.

mace. The reason for his state of mind lately wasn't a subject he wanted to talk about, even with his best friend.

"You need to get back out there, Canton."

At the look Canton gave him, his friend shrugged, gave him an "I tried" type of glance, spun around on his booted feet and left.

With mild interest he observed Ray as he made his way toward the woman, a predatory look on his face.

Canton twisted his large frame in the high-backed stool to face the bar. Six months ago he would have been doing the exact same thing as Ray.

He liked tall women, as he himself was six foot four. She *should* have been his type. She once *was* his type. Tall, leggy, sexy, blonde. He mentally ticked off the physical attributes she had that usually stirred his interest and libido. He glanced over his shoulder once more and saw Ray was talking with the blonde.

Just as Ray was now doing, Canton would have leaned down and been totally in her intimate zone. Would have given her *whatever* smooth words she needed to hear to feel special, to know that the adult games he wanted to play with her had nothing to do with pool, darts or spades.

That she was special to him. That she was the one.

If only for this one night.

He would have crowded her in, given her a taste of the infamous Wilde charm, confident that he'd have her where he wanted. Would have led her away from the bar to wind up at either her place or one of the local motels for the night.

But lately, he hadn't been interested in any of that. Not since his father had passed away, leaving the care of Brick and Riley, his two younger siblings, to him and his brother Tiber.

His brother and sister weren't small children; they were something worse: teenagers. Riley, the youngest and the only Wilde female, was a senior in high school and Brick, his young brother, was in his sophomore year at the university.

Not to mention his breakup with a woman he'd once considered marrying. He knew that Ray, as well as his brothers, thought she was the reason for his state of celibacy, but he knew it wasn't her. He'd come to realize over the past six months that he had in fact dodged the bullet with his fiancée, Anne. Fate had stepped in and actually saved him from possibly making the biggest mistake of his life.

But even to himself, he didn't delve too deeply into what was at the core of his ennui, for lack of a better word.

Lately no woman had captured his attention long enough to make an impression on him. Not even long enough to bed her.

And although he and Anne had broken off the engagement, he knew that she was still there, waiting, wanting him to return. But under her conditions: not only that Canton move out of the family home, but that they buy their own place and also move the wedding date up.

There was no way in hell he was going to do that. His family needed him.

He soon found out why she was so hell-bent on moving the wedding date up.

Canton shook his head, throwing off the heavy thoughts and sting of malcontent.

Family came first. It was a part of the Wilde creed. It was a creed that his pop had drilled into Canton, as well as his brothers and baby sister. And if the woman who purported to care about him didn't realize that, well, then, he had in fact dodged a bullet with her.

His family meant everything to Canton.

Unknown to him, a smile creased his rugged features when he thought of the youngest Wilde, Riley. She was growing up so fast. Kicking and raising hell from the time she came from her mother's womb, she'd been as much of a Wilde from the moment she'd come into the world as his biological brothers.

And now, with Pop gone, all she had was Canton along with his two brothers to look after her. He and Tiber, the oldest, had made a promise to his father that they'd always look after her, that no one would hurt her. A promise he intended to keep.

Because *that* was what family did. Took care of each other.

It was amazing what responsibility did to a man,

Canton thought with a grunt. Made him grow up quick, fast and in a hurry. Also showed who the real deal was when it came to those who loved you. Separated the true from the fair-weather. But he wouldn't have it any other way.

Besides, after he ended it with Anne, he hadn't been interested enough in getting "back out there" with anyone. Not exactly soured on love, but damn sure a lot more cautious when it came to trust.

He glanced at his watch, ready to call it quits for the night. He really wasn't in the mood to get "laid" as Ray suggested. Casual sex was the last thing on his mind.

But until Ray decided what he was doing…or *who* he was doing for the night, he'd wait for his friend to give him the word before he left him to his own devices.

Still looking in the direction of Ray and the blonde, Canton knew it wouldn't be long before Ray gave him the go-ahead to leave.

Until that time… Canton took another long drink from the bottle, his glance casually strolling over the clientele, bored and ready to say screw it and leave. Ray was a big boy; he could handle his own business.

At that moment, Ray gave him the signal and Canton shook his head, one side of his mouth kicked up in a grin.

"Well, no sense in hanging around," he murmured to himself, and drank the last of his beer.

Just as he was ready to turn away and settle his tab, his glance caught that of a woman who stood near her seat at one of the small round high tables, near the bar. He hadn't noticed her before.

She turned to fully face him and their gazes collided. In the act of removing her jacket, she paused, the garment dangling from her fingers. For a long moment she stood there, simply staring at him with her large doe-shaped eyes.

From where she and the woman with her sat, in one of the few well-lit areas and a small distance from where he was, Canton could see her clearly.

Unlike the leggy blonde in the tight red dress and stilettos, she wore a pair of skinny jeans that molded round hips and a plump butt, and ended where she wore knee-high boots.

The shirt she had on beneath the jacket was simple, but man oh man what it did for her curves. Made of some type of clinging material she'd only partially buttoned, the opened collar dipped to a pair of truly beautiful, full breasts, the crests overflowing the top of her bra, just a bit. He wasn't close enough to get a really good look, but dear God... His glance slid over her, seeing how she'd tucked the ends of the shirt into her jeans, showing off a nicely nipped-in waist.

He raised his glance, back up the length of her body until he reached her beautiful round face.

But it was her eyes that got him.

Large, and from his distance appeared light

brown, or maybe it was just the dance of light that hit them that made them so. Either way, they had a slight tilt in the corner. A small round nose and full, luscious lips that, along with the shape of her eyes, gave her the appearance of a sulky child.

Her pretty cocoa-brown-colored skin reminded him of silken, rich, decadent dark chocolate... Canton wondered if her skin was as soft as it looked. His palms itched to find out. His fingers rubbed against his palms.

Her hair was swept on top of her head in a topknot of some sort, but ringlets of light brown curls framed her heart-shaped face, giving her even more of a look of a pouting adolescent.

Again, his gaze swept over her body.

But any hint of a childlike appearance was negated by her body. She had a body that could raise the dead.

He lifted his glance to meet her sultry eyes and felt his breath hitch and lodge in his throat.

She returned his gaze.

First, she bit the corner of her mouth, as though in deep thought, before tugging on the full bottom lip and finally letting it go.

Canton could not look away.

Goddamn.

Their glances held for what seemed like forever.

Then moments later, she smiled as though she'd come to some decision.

Timidly at first. One side of those ripe, full lips of hers lifted, slowly. Then the other.

Then it grew.

Naked of any color, besides a shine of gloss on her full lips, her smile was breathtaking. And damned if Canton could look away. No one, ever, had captivated him the way this woman had with just one look. A mutual exchange of nothing more than a glance and a smile.

He felt an answering grin lift the corners of his own mouth, upward.

Canton hadn't felt like this in a long, long time.

He felt...*light*, happy for no damn reason on earth besides looking at her.

His body hardened, every thing about him focused on *her*. His cock thumped against his zipper, hardening, reacting to *her*.

As though she knew his thoughts, her eyes dipped for a moment in a charming display of shyness before reconnecting with his, her pretty full smile still in place. The effect on his body was unlike anything.

His cock hardened to pain, but Canton welcomed it as though it were a homecoming of sorts.

Beneath the bright light, Canton could have sworn he saw color blossom on her cheeks. As though she knew what she had done to him.

The little vixen, he thought, as a laugh escaped his mouth.

She was his.

Right then, right there, he decided.

It made no sense, no rhyme or reason.

If he weren't so focused on her, he'd think of what Ray would say, think, if he knew.

Probably that Canton had lost his mind. Moments before, he'd assured his friend the last thing on his mind was a woman, one-night stand or otherwise.

He hadn't lied.

In a blink of an eye, fate had something else in mind.

He felt it in his gut. His Wilde instinct.

His family were firm believers and followers of the Wilde instinct. An instinct their pop had trained them, from childhood onward, to believe in and follow.

The Wilde instinct was a part of their DNA as much as the height and blue eyes all the Wilde men shared.

That same Wilde instinct told him in the far recesses of his mind to get out now, if he wasn't ready. Now, before it was too late.

He placed the empty beer bottle behind him, blindly, never losing eye contact with the woman.

He *was* ready. He'd never been so ready in all of his life.

"Girl, come *on*, loosen up, let's have fun! But that can't happen if you keep turning your nose up like that!" Alyssa Thomas groused to her best friend,

Naomi McBride, as soon as the skimpily clad, weary-looking waitress placed their drinks in front of them, collected the money and left.

"And for the love of *God, please*, take that jacket off! I swear if you fiddle with the buttons one more time…just *one* more time—"

"What? What will you do?" Naomi challenged.

Alyssa narrowed her eyes. "I'm gonna fight you like a man!"

That made Naomi laugh, as it had been Alyssa's favorite threatening phrase since they were children.

She snorted, shooting Alyssa a glance. "Really? And how long have you been threatening me with that?" she said and both young women erupted into laughter, remembering.

They'd been friends from childhood, ever since Naomi had stood up for Alyssa to the school bully. Not by fighting, but with her words, something Naomi was very good at doing.

At the end of her sophisticated tirade against the bully—well, she'd thought it sophisticated at the ripe old age of seven—the bully looked as though she were about to go "in" on both her and Alyssa, not impressed at all with Naomi's serious words.

So Naomi, with her young face set, hands on hips, told the bully that she'd "fight her like a man" if she ever looked like she wanted to beat Alyssa up again.

She'd no idea where the crazy threat had come from, she thought with a laugh. She'd been just as scared, if not more, of the class bully, but she'd forced the fear away as she stood up to the much bigger girl, not backing down.

Words were all she had, as she knew the girl could beat her up.

Even at a young age, Naomi had used her words as her sword. Either it was the crazy threat or the way she said it that made the bully back away, mumbling about how they'd better stay on *their* side of the playground. It had become Naomi and Alyssa's private laugh for fourteen years.

After sobering, Alyssa pinned her friend with her signature look. Naomi refused to squirm beneath her friend's piercing gray eyes, feeling like a specimen under a microscope.

"Quit staring at me like that. And giving me that cray-cray look of yours. Gives me the creeps," Naomi groused.

"What look?" Alyssa asked, feigning innocence, holding her cheeks taut as though holding back a laugh.

"You know what look. Don't even try it. The same look you probably give to one of the frogs in your lab, rubbing your hands together in glee, *right* before you start slicing into the poor little guy," Naomi mumbled, making Alyssa's tinkling laugh ring out.

Which in turn made Naomi grin. Her friend's light, infectious laugh could make anyone smile. Unlike Naomi's laugh, big and full, a laugh she'd

He turned to the bartender and nodded his head for another before turning back to face his friend.

"What the hell is that supposed to mean, Ray?" he asked, mildly interested in Ray's response. "Because I'm a Wilde, I have some obligation to screw any willing female?" he scoffed.

"Uh, yeah… Hell yeah, that's what it means," was Ray's unrepentant reply, forcing a rusty laugh from Canton.

Canton turned back and accepted the beer the bartender had placed in front of him.

"Well, if you don't want her…" Ray allowed the sentence to hang, his look a cross between hopeful for a chance at the blonde and disgust for his friend's lack of interest in the willing woman.

With a half grunt, half laugh, Canton nodded his head. "Go for it," he encouraged, with casual disregard.

Ray took one last swig of his own beer and laid it on the bar counter and turned to face him, a neutral look on his handsome face.

"Man, you need to get laid. How much longer are you gonna think about…stuff?" his friend asked, his voice as calm as his expression. "How much longer are you gonna hold on to—"

"I'm good," Canton interrupted, before his friend went down that particular path. "Go handle your business, Ray."

Canton chugged half his beer down with a gri-

always been self-conscious about. It was just so... big. Only a few had heard her full laugh, and even fewer had made her laugh that way.

"Poor guy, huh? You know, if you want to be a doctor, you're going to be doing a whole lotta dicing yourself. And not on anything so mild as a frog's anatomy!"

"Yeah, but I'll be in the biz of *healing* and helping children...not dissecting and *murdering* innocent amphibians!" she quipped, and both women chuckled.

"Really, with that vivid imagination of yours with the whole 'rubbing my hands together in glee,' as I 'murder' poor amphibians, on the real, girl, I'm truly convinced that you just might have missed your calling as a writer!" Alyssa said, and they both laughed.

"Listen, Ne Ne," Alyssa said, automatically calling her by her childhood nickname of long ago. "We are graduating in a month *and* it's your birthday!" She paused and gave Naomi a considering look before continuing. "Come on, girl, it's not every day a woman turns twenty-one! And you promised me on your birthday you'd—"

Naomi held up a hand to stall the rest of her friend's sentence. "I know, I know, I promised I'd loosen up and, well, umm..."

Alyssa cocked a brow. "And..." she said, allowing the rest of the sentence to dangle, waving a hand encouraging Naomi to continue.

"And find a man to deflower me," she said, clenching her teeth in an attempt not to laugh.

Alyssa gave up a combo half giggle, half groan at Naomi's words. "Girl, stop! No you didn't say 'deflower'!" Both women laughed outright. "And no I didn't mean it like that, I just meant have fun, loosen up and well…" Her voice trailed off.

"I'm waiting," Naomi broke in, when apparently Alyssa seemed hesitant to finish her sentence. Again she felt laughter ready to bubble forth. Maybe this was just what she needed. It had been a while since she had, as Alyssa said, loosened up.

Naomi was celebrating a momentous birthday, and she, as well as her friend, was finishing her senior year at the university, although Alyssa was older than Naomi by a year. Naomi had completed her undergraduate work in three years, shaving off a year, and Alyssa had completed her basic training in the air force for ROTC before entering the university. The two were as close as sisters, and had been since they were children.

"Besides, it's kinda too late for the whole 'deflowering' thing, if you remember?" Naomi reminded her friend.

"Girl, please…that don't even *count*. Didn't you know that if the first time wasn't any good, you get a do-over? What? Yes. A do-over!" she said, snapping her fingers together. "But that ain't none of my business, though!" she finished with a smirk and lifted her glass to her mouth and took a sip…staring at Naomi over the rim.

Again Naomi laughed.

"Well, be that as it may. My one and only time left a lot to be desired. And not only that, but I haven't even dated since then. Not that I've had all that much experience anyway," Naomi said with a glum look.

"And whose fault is that?"

"Doesn't matter. You know school comes—" Naomi replied, ready to shoot with her standard answer.

"First," Alyssa interrupted and filled in for her, raising a palm. "Yeah, yeah, I know. You've always got that answer locked and loaded, girlfriend, ready to fire. But you promised we'd celebrate your birthday and graduation. What better way than to find some sexy beast and let him have his way with you, oooh Papi give it to me," Alyssa quipped, making goofy kissing sounds as she pooched her lips out. Naomi groaned at the cheesy reference to her favorite, even cheesier, classic romance film, but had to laugh along with Alyssa at her crazy antics.

It wasn't that Naomi didn't want to loosen up, as Alyssa said, and have fun. She'd just always been so focused.

Besides, most of the boys her own age just didn't do it for her. They all seemed so…young.

She sighed. "I don't know, Lyssa. What if I do *it* and end up falling in love with said guy I do *it* with, quit school, stay around here in Wyoming, have a bunch of kids, and never fulfill my dream of being a doctor? Huh? Huh? What then?" she asked, half joking, half serious. It was one of her fears to stay in their hometown and do…nothing with her life.

"Really, Ne Ne? All that is going to happen? Girl, I swear you're going into the wrong profession. You should really think about becoming a writer!"

"Ha!" Naomi replied, taking a drink and settling back in her seat.

"Listen, I'm not saying you gotta fall in love with the first guy you get involved with or do *it* with!" She stopped and qualified the statement, as Naomi opened her mouth. "Reallllly do it with," she said, and Naomi grunted. "Girl, just do it, have fun and move on! Seriously, that's my motto. Ain't nobody got time for falling in love!" Alyssa chuckled at her own joke.

"Hmm. I don't know. Most of the guys I know just don't do it for me. At all. Not even a little bit," Naomi replied with a deep sigh.

Feeling warm, she stood up to take off her leather jacket, to which Alyssa shot her an approving look and mumbled, "Finally!"

"And I think you've been reading those romance books of yours way too much. Trust me, if it were that easy to find Mr. Right, I would have been married with a bunch of kids a *long* time ago! And besides, what if that did happen, would that be so bad?

Tall, dark and fine could be just the ticket for you! Have a hot, sexy brief affair, release some of that tension you carry around like a bad habit. Hmmm." Alyssa stopped, a thoughtful expression crossing her small gamine features as she took a sip of her drink, lost in thought.

Naomi was contemplative when her friend grew quiet, and she removed her jacket, feeling warm and actually more comfortable than she thought she would feel.

Maybe Alyssa was right.

Maybe a fun rendezvous was all she needed, with a tall, dark— Her thoughts were cut short when she looked up, her jacket in her hand, and met the cornflower-blue eyes of one of the hottest men in Wyoming, Canton Wilde.

She swallowed, hard.

Although she was younger than Canton by at least three or four years, Naomi knew of him. Heck, every female under the age of ninety-nine in and around Cheyenne knew of Canton, as well as his siblings. Not only were they one of the richest families in the area, if not the richest, the men were so hot, so sought-after, they could all collectively star in their own reality show, of the *Bachelor* competition variety.

Tall, he had to be over well over six feet, easily a full foot taller than her own five feet four inches.

From where he stood, the light from the bar

showed his full body, face and all. But in reality, Naomi knew what he looked like from memory.

He wore his dark blond hair closely cropped to his well-shaped head, while a stubble of a beard the same dark blond shade shadowed his chiseled squared jaw. His long nose was aquiline. And she knew that the slight bump in the center, he'd gotten being tackled in high school while playing football.

Her glance slid over his beautiful male form.

Casually, he wore jeans that sculpted and hugged his thick thighs and muscular legs. The light from the bar seemed to focus on the center of his jeans, and his zipper, and the distinct bulge thereabouts. Or maybe it was her own lust that had her helplessly gazing at the man's crotch like some kind of wanton woman.

Whatever it was, helpless, she stared at him, transfixed. She forced her gaze away and met his eyes, his glance hot and filled with something she dare not name…

Was it her imagination, or was she really seeing what she thought she was seeing? Naomi wondered, wetting her lips with a quick swipe of her tongue. And if so, then…dare she?

Why not? she thought, a plan forming in her mind. Why not…proposition Canton Wilde? Not as if it hadn't happened to him before; she well knew his rep. Besides, who better to really, uh, deflower her than him, she thought, feeling bolder by the millisecond as she allowed the wild thought to marinate in her mind.

She bit her lower lip, wondering if she *dared* to be so bold?

Naomi let go of her lip and smiled.

It was small at first. Just one side of her mouth kicked up.

The stronger the thought took root in her mind, the naughtier, the bolder, she felt.

Empowered, even.

Now both sides of her mouth lifted up, until a full-toothed smile took over her face with a mind of its own.

His bright cornflower-blue eyes widened, and his own very sensual mouth lifted in the corner. Naomi just about melted right there on the spot. Dear God, the man was beyond sexy. He oozed sex appeal like other men sweat.

Question was, did she have what it took to actually go through with what was fermenting in her mind?

They held each other's gazes, communicating on some odd, unique wavelength that was new, fresh, exciting. One that only they felt, only they knew about.

It was as though they were sharing some secret of the universe that no one else could claim.

The club, the noise, Alyssa, all faded away as she held Canton Wilde's penetrating, hypnotic deep blue gaze.

Her nipples hardened beneath her gauzy blouse.

As though he knew, though there was no *way* he could tell from their distance away from each other, Canton's gaze wandered, briefly, to her breasts before returning to her eyes.

She inhaled a swift breath.

Naomi couldn't have looked away had her friend told her the club was on fire.

Chapter 2

"But then again, would it be *sooo* bad meeting Mr. Right? How romantic would that be… I mean sure, you'd have to stay in Wyoming, but then again— Uh, Naomi?"

Naomi was oblivious to the small fingers being snapped in front of her face. "Girl…are you even *listening* to me? Naomi?" Now frustration flavored her friend's tone.

Alyssa stopped her monologue and stared at Naomi, still snapping her fingers in front of Naomi's face in an attempt to get her friend's attention.

Naomi tore her gaze away from Canton and turned her focus to her friend.

"Huh?" she asked, feeling completely unglued.

Naomi had no idea how long she and Canton Wilde had exchanged that long, intense moment.

For Naomi, it felt as though time had stood still. Unconsciously, she brought her fingers to her forehead to wipe away the sweat she knew just *had* to be there.

Dear God, the man had brought her to a heated mess with just a look. But it was more than a look. It was a sensual exchange, the likes of which she'd never experienced.

"Girl, ummm, are you okay?" Alyssa asked, a look of concern etched on her pretty face.

"Yeah, I'm good… I, just, uh, was checking out everything," Naomi murmured, trying to gather her wits about her enough to form a coherent reply. "That's all," she replied, forcing a casual smile. "So this is game night, huh? Looks like fun!" she went on, completely flustered from her exchange with Canton Wilde, but trying desperately to adopt a cheerful facade for her friend. "I should have let you bring me here before! Of course, as I'm just now legally able to, I guess that couldn't have happened, huh?"

Naomi clamped her mouth shut, feeling as though she were blabbering. Nerves. That's all it was.

Rattled nerves had her blabbering incoherently, sweating and acting crazy.

She offered Alyssa another shaky smile, hooked

her jacket over the back of her bar stool and climbed back onto the high-backed chair.

She hastily lifted her drink from the table and brought the cool glass tumbler to her lips.

Alyssa was watching her carefully, a concerned look on her face.

"You sure you're okay?"

Naomi waved her concern away with a flip of her hand as she took a healthy swallow of the drink Alyssa had ordered them.

The alcohol smoothly went down, the taste a curious blend of sweet and sour; oddly mellow, and *very* good.

Moments later, the liquid began to burn her throat slightly. But it was too late; Naomi had drunk half the glass before she realized its potency.

She scowled and placed the drink on the table, and gave her friend a *look*. "Girl, what in the world did you order for me?" she asked with a squeaky voice, the strength of the alcohol compromising her vocal cords temporarily.

"Oh, it's not that bad! It's just an apple martini. They're delicious!" Alyssa replied, and to prove her point took a healthy swallow of her own.

With a lifted brow Naomi watched her friend try to fake the funk and pretend the drink wasn't strong.

She gave her friend kudos when she held her own, only giving a slight grimace, but still had to tease her. "Uh-huh, right!"

"Well, I thought it was innocent!" Alyssa said, holding back a laugh. "But, look, it came with a little umbrella. How could anything be bad that comes with its own little parasol?" Ever the comedian, she lifted the tiny drink accessory in her hand and twirled it around. "Awwww…see, isn't it cute?"

"Yeah, sure, Lyssa. It's about as cute and innocent as a baby rattlesnake," Naomi replied drily.

"You know, the drinks they serve here on game night are known to sprout hairs on your chest. If you're not used to strong drinks, you might wanna stick with a Shirley Temple."

Naomi swiveled in her chair and nearly fell out of her seat when she glanced up, way up, into the eyes of Canton Wilde.

When she toppled forward, but before she could actually fall, he was there, big hand cupping her elbow, steadying her.

"You okay?" he asked in his deep, sexy-as-hell voice.

Large, sculpted, beautifully defined muscles were revealed in the short-sleeved checked shirt he wore as he held on to her arm. In reflex, she grabbed his forearm to steady herself, feeling the ripple of coiled masculine strength beneath her fingertips.

Naomi barely repressed the desire to hold on and never, *ever* let go. She bobbed her head up and down, robbed of speech when he asked her again if she were okay.

Girl, get yourself together, she mentally chastised herself.

"Yeah, um, I'm fine," she said, not speaking much above a whisper, and she didn't think he heard her in the loud club.

"Yeah, you are," he replied.

Startled, not thinking she heard right, Naomi's eyes flew to his, and she flushed at the look in his stare.

The clarity of his meaning shone brightly in his gaze, and Naomi knew he was the one.

Standing so close to her, Naomi could *smell* him. Her eyes nearly feathered shut at his appeal. His cologne was lightly woodsy, blending with his own natural scent, which made for an intoxicating aroma.

She inhaled deeply, taking in all of him, everything feminine in her coming alive as she reveled in his unique masculine scent.

Naomi made a bold decision.

One she probably wouldn't have made had she been (1) completely sober, and (2) not goaded into a rash act by her friend's meddling.

Actually, in her heart Naomi knew that Alyssa had nothing, absolutely *nothing* to do with the decision she was making. The decision to claim Canton Wilde for the night.

Just one night.

"May I?" he asked, interrupting her scandalous musings.

"Yes, um, of course," she said, without looking or asking Alyssa if it was okay for him to sit with them.

In all honesty, Alyssa had all but vanished from her mind and thoughts.

Which was why she didn't notice the "shit-eating grin," as her daddy would call the look on Alyssa's face. Or her mumbled excuse to leave the table, to go say hi to a "friend" she saw across the bar.

For Canton and Naomi, there was no one else but the two of them. He sat across from her and placed his hand over hers and she shivered.

"Before I ask to buy you a drink, will you share your name?" he asked, a deep dimple creased just one cheek, and Naomi nearly groaned aloud at the sexy characteristic. "Can I buy you a drink?" he asked.

She shook her head and offered a slight grin.

"No, you won't tell me your name, or no, I can't buy you a drink?" he asked, and her grin widened.

"No, no! I mean, yes, you can ask my name, but no, I have had enough. I, um, think I need to keep a clear head around you, Canton Wilde," she said and nearly bit her tongue out when he widened his eyes.

"I'm at a disadvantage, apparently. You know mine, but I don't know yours," he said, the small smile still in place, and she relaxed.

"It's Naomi. Naomi McBride. And I, um, I know about you and your brothers. Your sister, too. I mean, who doesn't know about you? I mean, the Wildes. I mean—"

She stopped, and clamped her mouth shut. If she said "I mean" one more time, she'd find a way to kick her *own* ass...

He laughed outright.

Hmm. Naomi barely held back a moan. The sound of his full laughter caused several people around them to turn and look. The closest table was a group of women, who all gave Canton a head-to-toe, in-depth once-over. Something Naomi was sure he got a lot. The man was fine with a capital *F*.

The fact that he was looking only at her, and not giving the table of ogling women any notice, made her smile brighten just that much more and her confidence kick up another notch.

"Well, if I can't buy you a drink, how about a dance?" he asked, grin still in place on his *fine* face.

The thought of being that close to Canton, his unique scent washing over her, brought a fresh rash of goose bumps slithering over her entire body.

Naomi was hopeful yet nervous of what *might* be...

She made a promise to herself right then that before the night was over, if she had her way, they'd be doing a lot more than dancing.

Naomi nodded and smiled, meeting his hot blue stare, his eyes searching hers for what, she had no clue. She drew in a ragged breath as she held his gaze before she placed her small hand within his much larger one.

As he led her to the dance floor, she gave no protest when he drew her body close, so *tight*...she felt the length of his hardness, his girth against her stomach. She swallowed. Oh, my...

As he wrapped his strong, muscled arms around her slim waist, without thought or hesitation Naomi brought her hands up to rest on his hips, her fingers casually twisting around the loops of his belt while her head rested against his rock-hard chest.

The beat of his heart strummed strongly, deeply, against her ear. Even his heartbeat was purely masculine.

Hypnotic.

She allowed her eyes to drift close.

Chapter 3

Seven years later

Canton Wilde leaned back against the antique brass railing surrounding the wraparound porch, crossed his big booted feet one over the over, and observed the woman he'd been watching for over fifteen minutes.

His attention was fixed, unwavering on the woman. With little thought to the brisk air besides lifting the collar of his worn plaid shirt, Canton continued his observation of her. She appeared to be in the midst of fighting a losing battle with the seat belt inside her old Jeep. Even though he was a distance away, Canton could clearly *feel* her irritability.

A chuckle erupted from his mouth.

He shoved away from the railing.

Canton wasn't sure if it was the surprise of his own chuckle, one he admitted, if only to himself, was a rare thing to hear. Or if it was the sight of the woman as she finally emerged from the Jeep that made him catch his breath and push away. Once he got a good look, his Wilde instinct kicked in...it was more of the latter than the first.

He narrowed his eyes and leaned back again, at an angle that placed him away from her line of vision should she glance his way.

Damn if he even knew what in hell had made him stop in the first place. He'd intended to grab something to eat and a beer at the end of the day, tired as hell and pissed off at the latest load of crap he'd had to deal with from Cyrus White, the representative from the Rolling Hills Corporation, a task he detested.

His older brother, Tiber, who like him and his siblings was part owner of Wilde Oil Enterprises, was also the family lawyer. Tiber was the Wilde who dealt with the other bigwigs, execs and lawyers alike. *Tiber* was the sophisticated Wilde. The Wilde who dealt with the likes of snakes such as Cyrus without wanting to wring his narrow-ass neck. Something Canton wished like hell to do. But he promised Tiber he'd refrain.

Tiber was all the things Canton was not. Refined,

tactful when need be, when dealing with other corporate types. A fact Canton was immensely happy about.

Until he'd had to take over for his brother.

He bit out a curse.

Tiber was out of country at the moment, so the job of acting CEO fell to Canton. He'd much rather be out on one of their oil rig sites with the men, overseeing the drill or working on one of the rigs right alongside them as he was known to do on occasion. Somewhere he'd be right now had he not had to fill in for his brother.

Being in the field with the men was much better than behind some damn desk dealing with corporate America.

If Canton had his way, he'd have nothing to do with either Cyrus or Rolling Hills. Neither the man nor the company he represented had sat well with Canton. Something was *off* about both. He always left feeling apprehensive and annoyed after any dealings with either. And he never felt that way when he was on the rig.

But at the last family meeting, he, along with his brothers, Tiber and Brick, and their younger sister, Riley, had decided that they'd hear the company out, after the board had given Tiber a report containing the preliminary offer. Canton, as CFO, had already gone over the numbers several times with their head of accounting.

After the family made a favorable decision, Tiber, who was at the time acting CEO of Wilde Oil Enterprises, was to be the contact for the Wildes with Rolling Hills.

That was before there was trouble with one of the Wildes' international accounts and Tiber had been forced to go overseas and handle the issue personally. Which left Canton in the position of temporary CEO until his return.

He uttered a disgusted grunt and mentally shrugged off the memory of his latest bout with Cyrus.

He returned his attention to the woman.

But...something about her had caught his attention, just as he'd been about to enter his family home.

He didn't really know how long she'd been there; could have been five minutes or an hour. He knew she hadn't seen him. Hell, he doubted she was aware of much going on around her from what he'd observed.

She'd been staring out her driver's window, away from the mansion, as she'd been parked at the very edge of the road. Slowly, she turned the ignition on. After a few sputters, hisses and coughs, the old Jeep crackled to life.

She drove so slowly up the winding driveway he wondered if she was someone who'd lost her way and was trying to figure out her next move.

But no one gained access past the gate guard and

this close to the Wilde family mansion without getting vetted.

So it was someone they knew.

Canton waited. He'd eased his large frame into a strategic position, one where he knew she couldn't see him until he was ready for her to see him.

Something about this intrigued him.

For the moment he forgot all about Rolling Hills and the disturbing little man who rubbed him the wrong way. His focus was all on the woman approaching his family's home.

There was something familiar about her.

The woman faced the front of the mansion. From Canton's distance he saw the determination and set of her shoulders as she hoisted her bag closer to her side, squared her shoulders even more, if that was humanly possible, and closed the door to the Jeep.

Damn, she was beautiful...

Fully emerged from the truck, she made her way toward the house, and finally, finally he could see her full body.

He dragged in a swift breath as the woman drew closer.

The soft sway of her walk and smooth curves gave new meaning to the word *stacked*.

It was cool outside, and she wore a classic hip-length white leather jacket with the belt cinched tightly. The ends were tied in a big bow, like a present, highlighting her small waist, nicely rounded hips and full, plump breasts. All clearly visible beneath her layers.

Hell, Canton thought as he watched the woman approach, a figure like hers couldn't be hidden or camouflaged behind anything so inconsequential as a jacket.

From his vantage point, he watched her approach. There was even something familiar about the way she walked.

Although the autumn air was chilly, the sun shone brightly and caressed her toasted brown skin, which seemed to glow even more against the stark whiteness of her leather jacket. The way the light bounced and flickered against her smooth skin brought more awareness to Canton.

At that moment the wind chose to blow, whispering air against her body, molding the soft leather jacket she wore even closer to her sinful curves, making Canton's body harden, tightening with every step she took closer.

His attention was riveted on the woman.

The wind again blew a gust of air over her. She wore her hair in a high bun, but tendrils of curls escaped and whisked across her face. The woman raised her face toward the sun, a half smile tilting the corners of her full mouth upward.

It was as though she and the sun were old friends, communicating. She remained in that pose for what seemed like an eternity. And Canton wouldn't have been able to look away had his life depended on it.

When she lowered her head, she continued her pace toward the door.

He knew he should walk away. Something was telling him to *move* his ass now, before she caught him.

Something told him if he didn't his life would never been the same again. That instinct he had, the same instinct he'd inherited from his rough and rugged father, the same instinct that he and his brothers and as their baby sister all shared, the kind of instinct that told a man in business when it was time to move, in poker when to fold.

The same instinct that was now telling him to turn and move away before it was too late. But damned if he could.

So he just stood there, watching her stroll closer to the house, to him. He frowned when he caught her lips working, as though she were talking to herself. She stopped, closed her eyes and performed the sign of the cross. He felt one side of his mouth quirk in a half smile.

She had no clue she wasn't alone, that she was being watched. Something told that if she did, she would be mortified.

She was stylishly dressed; he ran his gaze over her as she came closer. From the soft-looking leather jacket cinched tightly at her waist, over her curved hips in the calf-length leather skirt, down shapely legs, housed in knee-high boots, she was the epitome of sophistication. He wondered if she were from around Cheyenne.

Canton's frown deepened. She was so lost in her own thoughts, he knew that she believed she was alone.

But Canton observed her as she walked with determination in her stride, up the winding path that led to the house.

She was a woman on a mission.

Everything about her told him that.

He again felt that curious shift in his awareness. Whatever her mission was, that same instinct that told him if he wanted his life to remain unchanged he should run the hell in the complete and opposite direction, also told him that part of that mission she was clearly on would involve him.

She reached the front of the house and lifted her face, and it was then that Canton nearly gave himself away.

He had never forgotten that face.

He'd never forgotten the feel of those curves on that body...

His hungry gaze roved over her, head to toe.

She had one of the prettiest complexions he'd ever seen. Her heart-shaped face was the color of deep milk chocolate with a hint of cream. He had never forgotten the color or feel of her...

Large, light brown almond-shaped eyes stood out against the richness of her complexion.

But it was her lips that captured him now, as they had before. Neither had he forgotten how they tasted. Full, plump and delicious, they called out to him, beckoning him, daring him to taste their ripe lushness.

Just as they had seven years ago.

His body hardened, alert; like a hunter watching his prey, his gaze was unwavering.

And in that moment Canton knew his life had, *again*, changed forever.

He also knew in that moment that running was the furthest thing from his mind. And neither would he allow her to run this time.

Hell no. Not this time. Not ever again. His face, body and everything else about him tightened up.

A purely masculine gleam shone from his eyes as he pulled his hat down further on his head, shielding his eyes.

Hell no. She wouldn't get away from him this time.

Chapter 4

Naomi McBride cast a quick downward glance over her body, making sure she was put together well.

"I need to be on point," she muttered to herself as she made sure nothing was hanging out of place.

She smoothed nervous hands down her leather jacket, retying the ends, again, wondering for the one hundredth time if her outfit conveyed what she wanted: a strong independent woman, a woman no one, not even a notorious Wilde, would consider lightly.

A woman to be taken seriously.

She straightened her burgundy leather skirt over her hips for the third time while absently toying with the buttons of the white leather jacket she wore to combat the chilly Wyoming air.

A shiver coursed through her body while a sigh broke from her lips.

"I already miss Texas." She fiddled with the buttons of the supple leather jacket. "Whoever heard of it being cold in September?" Naomi shuddered and then stilled, forcing her fingers away and stopping the nervous gesture.

She turned back to face the mansion.

So cold, impersonal. Just like the heartless family who lived inside, she thought, refusing to acknowledge how the wraparound deck of the cold, heartless mansion really appealed to her.

Nor did she address the issue of her being unfair to a family that was never heartless to anyone. At least they never had been before. Now, well… she just didn't know. She'd been away so long, she had no idea.

Naomi inhaled deeply, a fortifying breath. She could do this. She had no choice. Her family had no choice.

Naomi wondered even now how long her family would have kept their situation from her? How long before one of her parents would have told her the family ranch was in jeopardy?

She sighed, thankful she'd kept in contact with her sorority sister and friend Althea, or who knows how long it would have been before she'd be made aware of their dire situation. Had it not been for Althea, it might have been too late to do anything about it. She smiled thinking of her friend Althea Hudson.

She mentally shook her head, correcting herself, as she'd just learned of her friend's marriage to a man from another set of Wildes, men ranchers living on their land just outside Landers, Wyoming.

She and Althea still needed to talk about *that*, Naomi thought. She'd been so out of the loop working at the pediatric center she hadn't known of her friend's marriage. Yet as soon as she'd said the last name Wilde, Naomi wondered about the connections between Althea's Wilde and *her* Wildes, not realizing the possessive and personal way she'd characterized the Wildes of her acquaintance.

But there was no time for investigating that now. Naomi had other pressing things to take care of.

Again, she shouldered her bag higher and closed the door of her Jeep with the curve of her hip.

"Robbing Peter to pay Paul, and Mary wants her money, too."

A sad smile lifted the corners of her mouth, thinking of what her mother said last night as Naomi was going over the family accounts and correspondences with Rolling Hills once again.

Naomi had sighed and pushed her small oval wire-framed glasses farther up her nose as she went over her parents' financial statement.

"I brought you some tea, baby," her mother had

murmured, and Naomi had glanced up to see her mother in the doorway.

With a tired smile, she'd pushed the papers away and shoved away from the desk. Walking over to her mother, she had wrapped her arms around her shoulders.

"We'll figure it all out, Mom. Don't worry. I won't let them take the ranch," she'd promised, and as her mother hugged her, the seed of dread grew even more in Naomi's gut.

She had to figure out a way to help her parents and save their livelihood. There was no time for nerves or fear to get in her way.

Brought back to the here and now, she glanced at the mansion in front of her, preparing herself for her conversation with Tiber Wilde.

Again, she thanked God that Althea had reached out, contacted her, worried about Naomi's parents and their family ranch. Althea had learned of Naomi's parents' inability to pay the back taxes on their small ranch.

Unfortunately the taxes weren't the only issue the McBrides were facing, Althea had told her, knowing more about what was going on with Naomi's family than she did.

Rolling Hills Corporation, the same mega conglomeration that had *attempted* to threaten Althea's Wildes with a takeover, among other dubious business attacks, had been buying up small ranches in and around the area. The fact that it had its eyes on the McBrides' property was a fact that most in the area knew.

A little more digging between Althea and her had unearthed more troubling information. Naomi had learned that unless her family came up with the money to pay the taxes, the ranch would go up for auction and Rolling Hills would have its greedy hands out, ready to snatch up her family's livelihood.

The final piece of information had uncovered a link between Wilde Oil Enterprises and Rolling Hills Corporation, and that's when Naomi's heart had sunk.

Not only were her parents behind on the taxes, but also recently, someone had purchased the tax lien certificate for their small ranch. Which meant, in essence, on top of the back taxes, her family would be obligated to pay an interest fee on top of the money they already owed.

Naomi had put the mountain of paperwork away late last night, before she'd unearthed who'd bought the tax lien, so she could sleep. She needed to be fresh today for her meeting with Tiber Wilde. However, she had her suspicions about who had bought the tax lien: Rolling Hills.

At the end of the day, her family's situation was dire. Nerves already stretched taut as the strings on an out-of-tune guitar nearly snapped when she realized her best bet would be to contact the Wildes.

For her parents, Naomi would do everything in her power to help them.

What was wrong with her, anyway? She hadn't been this nervous since...she frowned, her brow furrowed, and she immediately rejected the memory to surface about the last time she'd been this anxious.

In *recent* times she didn't know the last time she'd been this panicky. Then again, she couldn't remember when she'd felt so...helpless, such a lack of control.

A whisper of memory diverted her attention briefly, again, refusing to be silenced, bringing to mind that *other* time. A time when she'd been tense and plain old silly as hell.

She'd felt all the sophistication of a child. She shook off the memories.

She hated that feeling. The feeling that she had no control of her own destiny. There was no way she'd have come to the Wildes had she any choice, but it wasn't just her life she had to consider, it was her family. And besides, she most definitely wasn't that silly little girl from seven years ago.

She sighed. If only her parents had told her what was going on, she might have been able to help them in some way. But they hadn't, and Naomi had no clue her parents had been struggling with the mortgage and trying to keep it all together. She had no idea they were behind in the payments. Had she known...

"But they didn't tell me, and now I'm here," she whispered.

But now…she shook her head. The fate of her family was up in the air. As soon as she'd found out she'd come home. To do anything else was not an option. Before she'd even come home, she'd begun assessing what was going on, and whom she needed to speak to, in order to help her family.

She'd found out the Wildes were involved and the ball of nerves in her gut grew. But she had no choice. Biting the bullet, she'd reached out and contacted Tiber Wilde before she'd left Texas and the soon-to-be-closing pediatric clinic where she worked. At least it was Tiber Wilde she'd reached, as he was the oldest Wilde and CEO of their company. Via email she'd made her initial approach, thankful when he'd agreed to meet with her when she arrived in town. They'd scheduled a meeting for today.

She'd been home less than a week and had hit the ground running. She had to save her family or go out trying. Because that's how the McBrides did it, she thought, straightening her back. Even if it meant confronting one of the notorious Wildes.

Again.

"Oh, Lord," she mumbled, that crazy nervous lump returning tenfold, forming directly in her gut.

At least it wouldn't be… She shut down the thought. Even thinking of him sent conflicting feelings and thoughts to run the gamut in her mind.

She felt heat engulf her face at the mere *thought* of that other Wilde brother, the one she hadn't seen since she'd fled Wyoming directly after she'd graduated early from college.

Far, far away, she thought with an embarrassed shudder.

She tore her mind away from all thoughts of the second eldest Wilde and reminded herself just why she was here: to try to save her family's small ranch.

But she still sent a glance upward, thanking God that she'd been dealing with Tiber.

She slowly made her way toward the mansion, frowned, recalling the last email from Tiber Wilde, a note that although succinct, still was encouraging. He'd invited her to come to their family home to discuss her family's situation. Yep. Definitely encouraging.

At least Naomi had chosen to see it that way.

Hopefully what she'd learned about the Wildes since her time away from home had been exaggerated.

Most things she'd learned from the internet, but also from the few friends she'd remained in contact with from home. Fascinating tales of the Wilde men and their exploits with women.

From the time she'd been old enough to know who the men were, she, along with everyone else in their small town, had known that their last name was truly a depiction of the men. Rough, rugged, and just plain wild...

But maybe the stories had been exaggerated, and the men had matured since last she'd seen them.

She could only hope.

Again she wondered at the connection between her Wildes and her sorority sister's Wildes.

Her Wildes were into oil, not cattle ranching as were Althea's, but that didn't really mean much. Somehow the men could be related.

But none of that mattered to her. The only thing that mattered to Naomi was saving her family. Leaving the south and coming back home to practice medicine had been the only choice she could make after her friend told her of her family's troubles.

She glanced around the front of the lavish, graceful mansion. Although the early frost had hit, the lawn was still beautifully, carefully manicured, luxurious and tasteful.

The Wildes were without doubt the richest family in Cheyenne. In fact, they were one of the richest families in all of Wyoming, including the other family of Wildes Althea was now related to.

Not that any of that mattered to her. She was here for one reason only, and even the thought of eventually running into *him* could not deter Naomi from her task.

Even after all these years, she had a hard time thinking about him, much less even saying his name.

"Just say the man's name," Naomi chastised herself, lips curled. "He's *just* a man," she continued.

"Canton." There, she'd said it.

She nodded and smiled as though she'd seriously accomplished something to be proud of. But for whatever reason, her ability to say his name made her feel good. Damn good.

One might even say victorious, she thought with a smug smile.

"Canton Wilde."

She said his name again. Just because she could.

As one of her favorite authors once wrote, she said it because she had the *testicular fortitude* to do so.

She giggled outright at her nutty mental quip.

Naomi placed a foot on the bottom step of the stairs leading to the Wilde mansion.

"That's what my momma named me. And what can I do for you, pretty lady?"

The rough, deep sound of a male voice brought Naomi's head up, her eyes flying to the man who stood less than five feet away.

Oh, God, no, no…she fought the urge to run.

She struggled with the reaction to shut it down right then and there, the fat lady had sung, curtains down…and run.

She knew there had been a possibility she'd see him. She just didn't think it would be this soon. Thought she'd have more time to prepare.

Nothing she'd learned on the internet, nor through the gossip line…nor her own long-ago memories had prepared her for this, for *him*.

Starting at big booted feet crossed over each other, her eyes thirstily drank in every devastatingly fine inch of him. Long, thick thighs encased in coarse-looking jeans, where the rough material couldn't disguise the musculature.

Her eyes darted over the thick bulge that pressed against his zipper. With *bold* insistency.

Hmm. Lord…a quake, a shudder of pure need, defiant of her refusal to remember, rushed over her. Naomi unsuccessfully tried to control the gaze that swept over his wide, hard chest.

Despite the distinct chill in the air, he wore no coat, just a thick plaid shirt, the type of work shirt she'd grown up seeing most men wear in Wyoming. A workingman's shirt.

He'd rolled the sleeves up to bare his arms from the elbows down, and she had to stop herself right then and there again from the need to flee.

His arms were thick, muscled like the rest of him, sprinkled with a dusting of fine dark hair.

Her helpless gaze traveled the rest of the way up, past his wide shoulders and broad, muscled chest, a chest where she could see, just above the white undershirt he wore, a sprinkling of dark hair, the same color as the hair on his forearm.

He wore his hat low, covering his head, but memory reminded her that his hair was a rich dark blond, the color at odds with the darkness of his arm and chest hair.

As well as the hair that grew in a part of him she refused to think about. Another tremble rushed over her as she suppressed the memory.

Her eyes met his.

It felt as though his cornflower-blue eyes were staring a hole directly into her soul as he racked her with his casual gaze.

She refused to give in to the need to fidget and avoid his penetrating stare. Naomi vowed not to let him know he was intimidating with his scrutiny.

Unsettling her so badly it was a wonder she hadn't melted into a puddle of nerves at his feet there on the spot.

I am a professional woman, she mentally chanted and reminded herself. *No longer that silly girl with a crush on a boy who didn't even know my name, much less remembered something so insignificant as a one-night affair...*

No matter how hot it got, or how far they went...

Maybe he wouldn't remember her, she thought, hoped and prayed. It was a long time ago, and she knew she was just one of many women he'd known. A lifetime ago.

Besides, he wouldn't remember her name. One time, seven years ago, surely—

"Naomi McBride. It's been a while." His deeply masculine, panty-wetting voice put a screeching halt to her aimless mental wanderings.

Chapter 5

Shocked, she widened her eyes, and stumbled back and nearly dropped her bag. Her fingers unconsciously clenched and unclenched repeatedly, tightening and loosening over the sinewy roped leather straps of the knockoff designer bag.

She could hear every beat of her own heart like a roar inside her ears, and felt as though it were going to leap out of her chest as it pounded away a mile a minute.

Thump, kick, thump...thump, kick, thump...

If she could be anywhere, God, *anywhere* but right here right *now*...she would give her last dollar to make it so.

But life wasn't that easy.

She swallowed, took a deep fortifying breath and briefly closed her eyes for a moment and glanced upward, for what seemed like an eternity until she met the veiled eyes, and shadowy face of—

"Ca-Canton?" she asked, her voice coming out as nothing more substantial than a squeak. Naomi cleared her voice and tried again, "Canton Wilde?" Nope. Still squeaking.

The higher her voice went, the higher the level of hysteria she felt, building, building, building…up.

But dear God, there was nothing, not one thing, she could do about that.

Coming to the Wildes, even contacting them, had taken more courage than Naomi thought she had in her. The only reason she felt she could handle it from the get-go was because the conversation was to be with Tiber Wilde. Not Canton.

And even with that, initially Naomi only wanted to deal over the phone with Tiber, but had agreed to come out to see him, personally, after her subtle investigation led her to believe Canton would be out on a rig somewhere, anywhere but here, she thought.

Damn it!

Her mind scrambled, trying to fill in the facts.

According to both Althea Wilde and Tiber, Canton was out of town, so she had little to worry about, at least for the time being.

When she had her correspondences with Tiber,

she had carefully verified, without raising any questions, that Althea was right about Canton's being away, and his brother had assured her of that detail.

Althea had in fact told her that Canton wouldn't be back in the area for a few weeks, according to gossip.

"You still do that?" he asked, startling her out of her own musings in his deep sexy voice. She felt a flush rush over her despite everything, an automatic response to him, one that time obviously hadn't taken away.

Naomi clenched her jaw and made eye contact with him, ruthlessly stamping down the response her body made to him. Nipples pulsing in direct harmony with the wild beat of her heart, and a lot more. She felt the heat burn her face.

She thanked God that because of her complexion, he wouldn't be able to tell how badly she was blushing, at least.

That was all it was. Just some crazy chemical reaction, she assured herself.

"Do what?" she asked, clearing her throat.

"Reason things out in a conversation with yourself?" he asked, amusement tingeing his deep voice. "And blush as though you've embarrassed yourself?"

Her eyes flew to his, her hands reaching to cover both of her flaming cheeks. How could he tell she was blushing? she wondered.

"If I recall correctly, we met once before. Your folks own the McBride ranch, correct? Dean and

Roslyn McBride?" he asked, his expression inscrutable.

All Naomi could do was bob her head up and down in affirmation. Mute as a mule.

For a moment she could not say one dang word had her life depended on it.

It then dawned on her after all of his sentence sank in that maybe he didn't remember their one night all those years ago. Maybe he remembered her from her folks!

Dear God, please let that be it, she silently prayed.

"What are you doing here? I thought I had time, I, uh, I mean—" She stopped speaking, realizing that she was both blabbering and talking herself into a hole.

The same hole she wanted to bury herself in and throw away the shovel.

She clamped her mouth shut. Although she knew the chance of seeing Canton was there, she'd thought time would be on her side and it wouldn't be anytime soon.

Apparently time and fate were most definitely not on her side.

"What I meant was, I thought I would be speaking with your brother Tiber. He assured me that I would be dealing with him. We had an appointment today, to discuss my family's, um, situation," she continued, trying to get it together. "I'm here to discuss a possible resolution on behalf of my parents."

"Yes, I'm aware of the situation. However, Tiber isn't available. Had me pinch-hit for him," he replied, the tone of his voice inscrutable, making it hard for Naomi to discern his thoughts. "But as I said he filled me in on the situation. I just didn't make the connection on which family it was. Not until now." His odd wording made her wonder, again, if he remembered their intimate encounter, or if he simply remembered her from years ago, when she'd lived in the area.

Did he remember that night? The question ran through her mind like a never-ending merry-go-round. One part of her was secretly embarrassed if he *didn't*.

Because she had never, in seven years, forgotten one thing about their encounter. Not one thing.

Not the way he had looked, tall and commanding as he stood staring down at her as she lay before him, exposed, with nothing more than the thin silk sheet of his bed covering her body.

She could still see the look in his vivid blue eyes as he stood there, cock hard against his thighs, taking in every part of her body, making her wet before they'd even begun…

She drew in a swift breath. Even though she had tried to bury it, pretend it hadn't happened, her subconscious was always there to remind her. Like clockwork. For seven years. It would wake her up occasionally with very vivid dreams reminding her… that she'd wanted *so* much more.

Her breath caught in her throat; unconsciously, she held it for a fraction longer than normal.

He just stood there, staring at her, his look completely unreadable, and again she wondered...had she not even made an impression on him?

"I can wait. I mean, I can wait until he gets back. It's no biggie," she began, rambling, just trying to get it out without making a complete ass of herself as she began to walk backward. "I mean it *is* a biggie, it's my family. I just meant—"

"I know what you meant."

She exhaled the breath and slowly dragged in another; his unique scent, familiar after seven years, rushed over her. It hadn't changed. Just as he hadn't.

Her eyes fluttered, partially closing, and she stumbled slightly, unsteady and shaky.

Canton moved as though to steady her, his fingers barely making contact with her elbow.

With just that one touch, a barely there touch really, a thousand memories washed over her.

Her hand reached out to touch the slight stubble on his lean cheek, unknowingly making the contact, and his hand covered hers. His jaw was rough with a few days' worth of growth.

She remembered the feel of his jaw against the sensitive skin of her inner thigh...

His nostrils flared as she held his glance. His face lowered as though to kiss her, and it snapped her out of her odd trance.

Embarrassed, Naomi recoiled as though he had struck her, her hand falling away from the shocking contact.

A flood of heat flushed her cheeks and she glanced up to see his face had lost the temporary softening and again the unreadable expression was stamped across his handsome features.

"Well, you're stuck with me. And if I were you, someone needing a *favor*, I would be a lot more... amiable." The words mild, but the delivery, his expression and tone, were hard, impossibly so. And they hit hard, just the way he intended them to, she knew.

It felt as though he'd doused her with cold water. Naomi nearly recoiled again, feeling his rejection as though it were a physical thing. She barely stopped herself in time.

The look in his eyes wasn't dislike. It wasn't pleasant, either.

It was neutral. As though he didn't care one way or the other what her decision was.

Amiable? What did he mean by that?

Naomi composed herself and placed a calm expression upon her own face, striving for some level of professionalism. Fine. If he could do it, so could she. Besides, she'd only come here for her family.

She'd make a deal with the devil if she had to, to help her parents out.

She made eye contact with Canton again.

He'd shoved the cowboy hat he'd been wearing just the tiniest fraction farther down, as though purposely trying to hide his face from her.

His eyes peered at her, and though his face was shadowed, the hard lines of his squared jaw tightened and for a moment she felt his anger.

She shuddered.

She had to be imagining things. He probably didn't even remember her, much less be angry about something that happened so long ago. It had been seven years ago, and the encounter fleeting.

Wasn't nothing to trip about, she affirmed within her own mind. *He* wasn't anyone to trip over.

A voice in the back of her mind laughed, mocking her. She brushed it aside. Forcefully. As had become her custom whenever it reared its ugly head.

Either way, the way things were turning out, that might just be what she'd be doing: making a deal with the devil.

Canton opened the door to his home, and as casually as he could, walked inside. He left the door ajar for her to follow. Or not.

The decision was hers.

Before the door closed, he *felt* her hesitancy before her small hand moved and grabbed the doorknob. She pushed it farther open as she followed him inside.

Irritated with himself for being so hyperaware of her, he forced himself to keep walking.

Seeing her after all these years had jolted him, memories slamming into him like a tsunami.

Or a sledgehammer.

He'd never forgotten her. Every moment of their encounter had been permanently etched in his brain.

He didn't know how much it had, until seeing her for the first time in seven years.

For a moment he thought she remembered him; hell, she had to. The look in her light brown eyes when her hand had risen to touch him. Right then and there, he'd wanted to kiss those luscious lips, attack and devour them…before he devoured the rest of her.

Damn it all to hell!

Ruthlessly, he shut down the flood of memories along with the feelings they wrought. Nothing but irritation was what he felt as he strode inside the house, his booted feet hitting the tile adorning the entry floor with angry precision.

He didn't have time to deal with this. It had taken several minutes, but his mind made the connection on who she was and what she was doing here. What she wanted from the Wildes.

And it wasn't to take a trip down memory lane with him. To explain why she left, without a word.

She was here begging for help for her family, not to see him. His brow furrowed.

"You can go in the library," he finally spoke, his

tone curt. "Second door to your right. I'll be there shortly. I need to take care of something first," he threw out over his shoulder, indicating with a brusque jerk of his head where she could go.

He barely refrained from telling her where the hell she really could go, his jaw clenching tight as he strode away from her.

"Um, well, okay. Thank you," she replied, her soft, hesitant voice echoing in the empty house.

Canton *felt* her hesitancy. Again, hyperaware of her. Briefly, against his will, he hesitated before forcing himself to continue to walk away.

Fuck! He mentally bit out the expletive, beyond pissed at himself. He did not *want* to care about her or her goddamn fear.

The fear and uncertainty she felt was palpable and he knew it was for her family. But right now, all he could do was get the hell away from her, if only for a few minutes, and get it together before he faced her again.

Maybe that wasn't such a good thing, he thought, as he heard the high heels of her leather boots as they tapped behind him on the tile. Maybe he should just hear her out, and as soon as possible get her the hell out.

From his side vision he saw her go inside the door that led to the library as he'd told her to, and felt a level of irritated satisfaction. At least he'd have a moment to get himself in check without her liquid brown eyes staring a hole into him.

Canton flipped on lights as he strode farther inside his family's home, thankful it was a Friday. For the most part, besides Trudy, their housekeeper, more than likely he'd have the house to himself.

Tiber was still out of the country, and neither one of his younger siblings, Brick or Riley, would be back home until Labor Day to spend a few days, Brick currently overseas, working with one of their customers, and Riley at the university, where she was preparing to defend her dissertation.

He mentally went over the information his brother had given him about the woman he was to meet. At the time, he had no idea it was Naomi; even as he'd glanced over the forwarded email, her name hadn't registered in his mind. He hadn't made the mental connection until she'd shown up.

He whipped out his phone and stabbed a finger at the email application. Scrolling through an assortment of junk and personal messages, he found the forwarded one from Tiber.

Rereading the email from his new perspective was a hell of a lot different than before. He and his brother had discussed how to handle the situation. Canton was to hear her out, see where her family stood financially, and offer aid if they needed, with no promises.

The Wildes had been active members of their

community since their father had bought the land nearly forty years ago. As one of the leading families in the community, they'd also helped their neighbors, no matter how small, if they could. Their father had instilled in the men the need to not only help family, but their neighbors as well, and the men had carried out the tradition after his death.

Which was one of the reasons Canton had not completely come on board with having business dealings with Rolling Hills. They'd been aware of how it'd been slowly buying up many of the small ranches around the area, leaving fewer and fewer family-owned farms and ranches.

Neither had Tiber been on board, he knew, judging from the scattering of small ranches his brother had been quietly collecting the tax lien for, in an effort to save various families from those who could and would buy the liens and force payment immediately.

The McBrides were one of those families Tiber had instructed Ruby, their accountant, to purchase the lien for, once the family had been in default on it the previous year.

He'd keep that particular bit of information to himself for the moment.

He scanned her email to his brother, paying closer attention than he had before. Reading it again, slower, knowing the author of the email was Naomi.

Before, it had just been some anonymous woman

asking for help for her family; he'd had a completely different vision of this woman in mind.

Deep in thought, he pocketed his phone, a frown creasing his brow. She was asking for the Wildes to hold off, and asking if they had any clout when it came to Rolling Hills. If so, could they petition on her family's behalf? She said it was only for a time. Give her family enough time to come up with the money to pay the back taxes on their ranch.

It was then that Tiber had responded. Tiber, his stern, iron-and-steel, hard-core CEO brother, had agreed to listen to Naomi McBride and had given Canton permission and instruction to help her in any way they could; it was a family in their community, and as most knew, a Wilde helped a neighbor in need.

Although she hadn't given a dollar amount that her family owed, Tiber had easily found out, as the Wildes owned the tax lien, and the amount was negligible. At least to the Wildes it was. Hell, Canton could write a check for the amount from his own "piss in the wind" account as he called one of his personal accounts.

He could give her family the loan from any source—his own personal money, or from one of the family accounts—and not miss a beat and they'd be out of hock.

But this was personal. She was personal. And he'd be the one she would need to appease, the one she'd have to ask…to beg.

He yanked open the fridge, but hesitated, his hand automatically reaching for a beer, hovering. He grabbed a Coke instead, knowing he needed a clear head dealing with her.

Canton withdrew a second one and got down two glasses and placed them on the counter.

His glance went toward the covered dish where their housekeeper had made a lemon pound cake.

Hell no! A drink was all he'd offer her. She wasn't going to have him playing the nice host, Canton thought in irritation as he grabbed the drinks.

A purely masculine grin stretched his lips as he strode with a new purpose in mind toward the library.

If anything, by the time he was done with her, playing nice would be the tip of the iceberg of what he had in mind to do with her.

Chapter 6

While Naomi waited for Canton to return, she became a mass of nervous energy.

As soon as she'd opened the opulent, partially stained glass doors, she'd slipped inside and briefly leaned against them.

Then, realizing the expensive, intricate stained glass probably cost as much as she owed in student loans, she'd hastily moved from her leaning position.

It had taken a few minutes for her gut to stop churning enough to take in her surroundings.

He'd directed her to go inside the library, and she hadn't known what to expect; she equated a home library as being the same as a den, truth be told. But this was taking the family den to the nth degree.

The Wilde family library was stunningly gorgeous, a curious mixture of opulence, comfort and contemporary design, its built-in shelves filled top to bottom with what looked like thousands of books.

It had the bookworm in Naomi eager to investigate.

Her fascinated gaze danced across the room. For a minute she felt like a child in a playroom filled with all of her favorite toys.

A beautiful wrought-iron masterpiece of a chandelier hung from the high ceiling, filling the room with an amber-like soft glow. Illuminating enough to read in, but not harsh enough to interfere with the natural ambience the room seem to generate.

Thick crown molding along the baseboard of the room matched the molding along the ceiling. Three of the four walls held a massive load of books within their shelves, but one of the dark wood-paneled walls was more ornate with its molding, arched and recessed, with a set of stairs that led to a *second* tier of books for the reader to explore.

Completely beautiful and absolutely mind-blowing, the room's lavishness kept her mind busy for a moment, taking it off the issue of her current predicament, and one Wilde man named Canton.

She sighed deeply, running a reverent hand over the spine of a few of the books before one particular tome caught her attention. It appeared to be an antique Bible, from the gold embossed cross on the spine.

Gingerly she removed the leather-bound book. Her mouth formed a perfect O as she glanced over the cover.

Just like the spine, the cover of the antique book was embossed with gold lettering, simply designed yet beautifully crafted. Carefully she opened the thin vellum pages, leisurely examining the contents of its mounted illustrations and plates.

After delicately turning the pages, she noted the early 1900 copyright date and the illustrator's signature.

The same fear she'd had with the stained glass doors to the library, she also felt with the cost of the antique book she held. It alone could wipe out her student loan debt from medical school. Of this she had no doubt.

"My family has long held an affinity for collecting rare tomes, as well as contemporary types of books."

Startled when she heard Canton's sexy, deep voice, Naomi spun around on her heel, Bible in hand.

She warily watched him as he walked inside the room, closing the double doors behind him.

Before he'd entered the large, opulent room, Naomi marveled at the sheer amount of space. Suddenly, the walls seemed too close, the air too thin to accommodate his presence.

"That one in your hand was bought at a silent

auction. For a considerable amount," he continued, nodding toward the Bible she still held, seemingly unaware of how his presence unnerved her.

"It—it's beautiful." Her voice was barely above a whisper, and she cleared her throat. She gave a small shaky smile and turned around to face the shelf. With a steady hand she replaced the Bible where she'd found it.

"Please, have a seat," he said, motioning for her to sit after she turned back to face him, with a much steadier smile in place.

Besides the wall-to-wall shelves filled to capacity with books, the large room had several seating options, including a large dark leather sofa, the deep mahogany color matching the stain of the wood lining the walls and crown molding.

There were three other seating choices. One was two beautiful overstuffed brocade chairs, which appeared to be classic pieces, nothing one could find in any modern contemporary furnishing store.

The chairs flanked a low, elaborately carved octagonal table that just like the rest of the lovely furnishings was unique, and no doubt ridiculously expensive.

In the far corner nestled near the fireplace, was a decadently gorgeous, oversize chaise longue that could easily hold two people with a throw blanket casually tossed over the foot.

The library was as warmly inviting as it was classically beautiful. Her eyes stole back to the fireplace, and for a moment, she pictured herself in front of the fire, stretched out on the chaise longue with a glass of wine.

"If you like, I can start a fire," he said drily, dark humor in his voice, and she blushed, feeling as though he'd read her mind.

"No, no. That isn't necessary. But thank you," she said, infusing a brusque tone into her voice to stamp out the crazy momentarily longing.

"I brought you something to drink. It's just a Coke. Hope this is okay, but if you'd like something stronger let me know." He held out the tumbler of iced Coke and she stared at his big hand wrapped around the glass, the sprinkling of hair on his knuckles sexy as hell to her.

God, she had it bad, she thought in disgust.

"No, that will be fine. I don't drink," she replied and blushed at the look he gave her. "Well. Not much, anyway," she qualified her statement, feeling her face grow warm. That night seven years ago she had drunk. And drunk well.

Again, she wondered if he remembered. Naomi smiled stiffly and accepted the drink.

"Well, let's get down to it, shall we?" she said, taking matters into her own hands.

"By all means," he replied, his voice only slightly dry. "Let me pull up the documents I have on file and we can talk about your family's situation. Please, have a seat," he said, motioning for her to take the only seat near the desk. It was very close, and if she had her druthers, well, she'd stay where she was. But…she didn't.

He had home-court advantage, and she had to play ball the way he wanted.

She observed him, carefully, not wanting to miss a thing, not a nuance in expression or body language.

He placed his drink down on the desk once he'd reached it and sat down in the massive, gorgeous chair, propping his big feet up on the top as though it were a discount piece of furniture, and not the ridiculously priced piece she knew it had to be.

Naomi sat down in the seat he'd indicated, crossed her legs and then overlapped her hands over her bag she had placed in her lap.

She knew what he was reading; the carefully worded plea she'd written to Tiber Wilde, outlining the need to buy the lien back, and a carefully detailed payback schedule. She nervously rubbed her fingers together.

"I think you know what I came here for, and what I…my *family* is requesting. I need to know if you are willing to help us or not. If not then I understand," she began, only to see him haughtily hold up a hand as though to shush her.

No. No he did not… Naomi refrained from jumping up and slapping his arrogant, handsome face. No one shushed her. She was an educated, well-respected pediatrician. She was used to people giving her a little more deference than what he was showing her right now. How dare he shush her!

But for her parents...

The mental reminder was all she had. And the only thing that stopped her from telling his behind off, no matter how well defined and muscled it was, or how good it had felt as she'd held on as he'd plunged into her all those years ago... *Stop, girl. Just stop,* she mentally chastised herself.

If not for her parents she'd tell him where to take his damn help.

She held her tongue. Her momma didn't raise a fool. There was a time and place for everything.

For several minutes he perused the file, whatever file it was, and she remained silent, nerves taut, waiting for his verdict. Would the Wildes...would Canton Wilde help her family? She knew the fate of her family rested in this one particular Wilde's hands.

Or was he just allowing her to wait, squirm, only to dash her dreams, callously?

Longer moments went by, longer than necessary. He had to have already read the file, but was making her wait. She knew what he was doing...just as well as she knew what the faint scar looked liked that ran down the center of his well-cut abs. She'd never forgotten one thing about his decadently hot body.

She remained still, refusing to show him just how on edge she was.

"Okay, so here's the deal," he began, his deep voice ringing out in the quiet library making her jump. She sat up, spine straight, hands in her lap, and waited.

She focused her attention on him, her eyes locked with his. For all of her nervousness, fear and stress she felt for her family, she wouldn't allow him to see any of that. She was made of stronger stuff than that. The Wildes weren't the only family with steel running through their veins.

The McBrides were as determined and *just* as strong-willed as the Wildes.

A bit of her confidence returned. She knew in that moment that no matter what this man said, she and her family would be okay. He did not hold their destiny in his hands. Only God had that distinction.

As badass as he thought he was, he was no deity, she thought, feeling a tiniest bit of a smile lift her lips.

It was there that she saw it. The tiniest flicker in his eyes. He reacted to something, just now, and she saw it.

She was under no delusions. She was a smart woman. She realized he *had* to remember who she was. It was all there in his eyes. Eyes that promised retribution.

Slowly, he rose. Kicked back his chair, moved around the desk and sauntered over to where she sat. And stood less than a foot from her.

Naomi refused to move…

* * *

When she smiled it was over.

Canton had sat there, behind the oversize desk, pretending a nonchalance he was far from feeling, looking at the blank screen of his computer while mentally going through his plan once more, looking for objections she may have, thinking it through to make sure he knew how and what to do, to slyly counter any said objections.

Ultimately he knew he had her over a barrel. His ace in the hole was her love for her family.

Something Canton grudgingly admired about her. One of many things.

His plan was to get her out of his system one way or another. He admitted to himself that she'd played peekaboo in his thoughts way too often over the past seven years, and now it was time to exorcise the ghost of Naomi McBride once and for all.

And that was all she was. Nothing more substantial than a ghost. Someone of little significance beyond a whisper of something that once was.

Their affair had been fleeting at best, and one he shouldn't even remember, much less in vivid detail, but he recalled everything about that night. The way she felt, her soft skin against his, her legs wrapped around his as they'd made love for hours and hours… the memories were something that made no sense to him. Not the fact that he'd indulged in a bout of marathon lovemaking with her, but that he remembered it *and* her, and every detail about both.

He'd bedded women, had more than his share of protected casual sex. But there hadn't been one damn thing casual about the way she'd set his blood on fire from the moment they'd first met.

His plan had been to approach her situation with casual disregard. Outline her options. Tell her that in order for his family to try to help her family, she was going to have to earn it.

The way she would earn it would be to be at his beck and call, 24/7.

He sat on the edge of the desk and folded his hands, giving her his full attention.

"Here's the deal. The only reason I'm here and not Tiber is because my brother is overseas currently, handling one of our investments. In my brother's absence I am now the one who has to attend all the bulls—um, social events Tiber normally attends," he began, curbing his language but speaking as succinctly as he could, without giving her too much detail. "Events I don't normally go to."

Read as "social gatherings he normally avoided like the plague," he mentally corrected. He continued. "And I need someone to go with me. I'm…in between…escorts at the moment, and don't feel like dealing with what happens if I attend one of these events alone. You are the answer."

Although she sat still and never flinched or moved a muscle, he could feel her surprise and questions.

"I need an escort for these events. And that's where you come in," he said, trying to sew it all together as concisely as possible. "For the next two weeks, you are going to be, if only to the outside world, my current...escort," he finished, taking joy in the way her pretty chocolate-brown cheeks washed with a subtle hint of color, alerting him that she was blushing.

"And...and that's all? Me just escorting you to these social events?" she asked, frowning, biting the center of her bottom lip.

His gaze halted on her lips, watching as she worried that plump, succulent piece of flesh until he felt like groaning, his cock thumping against the too-tight confines of his jeans, the desire that had lain simmering for her rising to life.

Canton forced his gaze back to meet hers.

"Yes. That's it." The lie slid nice and smooth off his tongue. He didn't want to scare her. He felt her panic like a rabbit in a den of wolves, with him being the alpha wolf readying his prey.

He carefully watched her.

"And after the two weeks of me accompanying you on these...events, you and your family will do what exactly? And can we get that in writing...whatever it is, you're purposing? Just to make sure we are on the same page."

Another thing he liked about her—she was as intelligent as she was beautiful. The fact that she didn't bat an eye at what he was asking told him that she was under no delusions and knew that she was at his mercy. She either took the deal he offered, or she walked out of his home unable to help her family.

He inclined his head. "Of course. After we have reached an agreement, we can put in writing what we both agree upon." He actually liked her thinking.

It helped him. It was just a business deal. And when the business was concluded, their time would be over. And she would be exorcised from his thoughts.

"However, if all the conditions of the deal are not met, the deal is null and void."

She narrowed her eyes. "What other conditions are there?"

"When I need you…you come. No questions asked, no hesitating. If you want to save your family."

And like that, he made sure that she understood who was in control.

Chapter 7

"Well, do we have a deal?" he asked in a voice hoarse with suppressed emotion, an emotion that had no name, a mixture of anger, resentment, even as he tried to deny the underlying lust that still lingered.

He didn't know whom his anger was more directed at, Naomi for being the object of his feelings and lust, or himself, for feeling anything for her?

She bit at her lip again, hesitating, weighing the odds in her mind, he knew. He waited.

All he knew was that no matter what, he still wanted her. After seven years, and a fleeting time together...with no real fulfillment, not enough for him, he still lusted for her.

Through the years, as he'd been with other women,

he'd think of her. Not every time, and not with every woman.

But enough that he had never been able to forget her, an echo of her memory in the small corner of his brain.

He'd think of her at the most inopportune moments, usually when he'd least want to think of her. Thoughts, images of *her* beneath him, accepting him, all of him, bogarted their way into his brain, implanting the image of her face, one that he'd never forgotten, onto his current bed partner.

Only recently had her image began to fade the smallest bit.

And here she was, showing up in his life again.

But he had no illusions this time. For whatever reason, seven years ago he'd felt she was different, their connection different, special somehow. And when she'd left the next day, with nothing more than a note on the pillow saying thank you, he'd known what it felt to be used.

For whatever reason, she'd "chosen" him that night to bed. Not because she'd felt the same crazy connection that he had. Not because of anything other than plain old-fashioned lust. Nothing more or less. Something that shouldn't have affected him the way it did, but damned if it didn't.

Now he was determined to prove to himself that it wasn't anything to him, and neither was she.

He'd come to realize what it was: nothing but pure

lust. After a six-month hiatus from relationships and the breakup with his ex-fiancée, he needed good old sex. His libido had finally taken over, making his mind think there had been some cosmic otherworldly connection with her that hadn't been.

He knew now would be the opportunity to exorcise the seven-year demon of lust he'd had pent up until he'd had his fill and could forget her.

It made no sense. None of it made any sense. The *only* sense he could make of it was that he felt robbed. That night hadn't ended the way he'd wanted…or rather, the next day hadn't.

He walked nearer to her and reached out a hand. She hesitated, but eventually placed hers within his.

She rose, and as she stood there, staring up at him, fear but determination in her pretty light brown eyes, he felt something stir in his heart, something that he hadn't felt in a long, long time.

Damn it.

It was her. She was doing something to him.

He drew her nearer until he had her close enough that he could count each of the handful of darker freckles on her chocolate-brown skin. The fact that he knew she had them, that he had first discovered she had them when he made love to her long ago and she blushed, making them stand out, starkly, filled him with longing.

Canton had tried to get over the feeling of incompleteness, but could no more do so than he could stop the sun from breaking free and replacing the moon at dawn.

"You don't have to worry about your family. It's going to be okay. Everything will be okay," he said, gruffly, not even realizing he'd sought to assure her, to do anything to get that look of fear from her eyes, knowing she was deathly concerned about her family.

Tears filled her pretty brown eyes and he suppressed a groan.

And now, well damn, now she had him waxing poetic.

"Come on now, it'll be okay. But it's your decision."

"I…" She stopped and drew in a ragged breath to compose herself. "I'm just so upset about my folks… this lien on the farm is frightening, Canton."

Although his gut clenched, he forced himself to stay silent. To wait.

Then she bobbed her head up and down in agreement, a tentative smile on her face. He reached out a hand, brushed away at an errant spiral curl that escaped her topknot and placed it behind the curve of her small ear. Instead of moving his hand away, he kept it there, his gaze unwavering.

He expected her to recoil from him, as she'd done before when he had reached out to try to steady her. Instead, she held his gaze, and they both grew still, unnaturally so.

Canton couldn't have looked away, no matter how

damn badly he wanted to. On her face was the reflection of what was in his mind; mutual memories of a time seven years ago danced in the glow of her beautiful, unique light brown eyes.

The moment stretched taut.

As he waited to hear what she'd decided, it seemed hours but was in actuality little more than a few seconds.

"I, uh, I—" She stopped speaking and tore her gaze away from Canton's. His jaw tightened and eyes narrowed, but he carefully maintained a neutral facade.

No way in hell would he let her know how much it meant to him, her answer. It was purely a business proposition. He'd help her family, give them the time they needed, keep Rolling Hills off their backs, and in exchange, she'd give him…herself.

Whenever. However.

And there was no need for her to ever know that it was his family who held the tax lien against hers. That was information she'd never find out if he had anything to do with it, not until his time with her was over.

She eased away from his light hold, and his hands fell away. He watched her from hooded eyes as she walked over to one of the built-in bookshelves, her hand trailing over the binding of several volumes.

Her shoulders held a slight hunch, as though she felt defeated. The idea disturbed him for unknown reasons.

But within moments she straightened her back. Her head tilted to the side, and Canton knew she was having one of those one-way conversations again.

He felt an answering tug of one side of his mouth, a smile trying to break free, before he glanced away from her, irritated once again with himself for being so damn fascinated with her. Still, so turned on by her.

"And if I say no?" she asked, her voice small, uncertain, echoing in the large room. She partially turned to him, her head slightly over her shoulder, glancing back at him, yet not making eye contact.

Again, Canton felt a stirring of sympathy for her. Although in profile, her beautiful face, like her body, grew still, like a small bird afraid to take flight; her liquid brown eyes made his heart seem to stutter. He tightened his jaw and she turned back away from him.

He observed her as her small fingers traced over the spine of one of the books on the shelf, her body stiff and her back ramrod straight.

He made his way over to her like a magnet, without conscious thought, and now stood so close behind her he could again smell the essence of her wash over him like floral-scented rain.

"I… I don't know. I mean… I know what an escort is, I mean, *exactly* what all do you want from me?" she asked, her words barely above a hoarse whisper. "I mean, you could have anyone go with you to those functions as an...uh." She stopped, completely and obviously flustered and again flushed, something utterly beautiful to see against the deep color of her skin.

Canton moved his body boldly closer to hers, placed his hands on top of her shoulders and brought her body back against his so that her back was flush with his chest, her perfect ass nudging his thighs. He leaned in, closer, and rubbed the side of her face with his own.

The stiffness of his erection was a vibrant thing and there was no way in hell she couldn't feel it against her back. He was hard as granite.

But Canton had no desire to hide the proof of the fact that he wanted her, needed her.

He grasped her by the hips and pulled her flush against him, pressing her ass into his erection, grinding against her.

"Canton," she whispered his name, making him that much harder.

Her head fell back against his shoulder, a little moan escaping from her lush lips, and Canton felt moisture escape his cock.

Fully clothed, she had brought out something in him, feelings he hadn't felt before with anyone.

Just like her, the feelings she wrought from him were unique...and left him feeling off balance. Another first.

He turned her face so that he could get hold of

those beautiful lips of hers. It was a strange angle to hold her, but one that turned him on.

The act of holding her in this way, captive, with no way to maneuver away from his arms as he began to play with her, turned him on in ways he had never felt.

"I want you. All of you," he admitted around her lips, so far gone with lust he didn't guard his words.

Canton boldly lifted her silk blouse away from her skirt, deftly unbuttoning it before attacking the back closure at the waist of the skirt and easing the zipper far enough down so that the waistline was loosened.

In one smooth move he reached a hand inside the waist of her skirt, while the other unhooked the front closure of her bra and cupped one firm breast, messaging the heavy globe, fingers feathering over the tightening nipple.

His hand traveled down her waist and eased past her flat stomach until he reached her panties. Deft fingers slipped inside, moving the elastic band away before he found what he was looking for.

Her cry rang out loudly in the room.

"I think you want me just as badly, Naomi," he murmured against the corner of her full mouth, stroking her lips with his tongue, licking away at the moan that had escaped as his fingers caressed the lips between her legs.

His fingers were saturated with her dewy wetness. He'd found proof of his declaration.

Canton eased his fingers out of her reluctantly before he turned her around in his arms to face him.

His gaze locked with hers, daring her to look away, much less try to leave his embrace. She was so beautiful. The lust and passion had softened her features, her full lips made even fuller by his kisses.

He caught her half-repressed flinch as he placed his hand beneath her chin, drawing her face upward.

Keeping his gaze locked with hers, he brought his finger to his mouth and licked her cream from the digit, before he placed it on her lower lip.

He silently dared her to lick it as well. But he doubted she would.

She held his gaze, and slowly, so damn slowly, it was nearly a painful thing to watch, she brought out her tongue and swiped at his finger, the move bold and not expected.

Canton's hot gaze traveled over the bottom curve of her lip, outlining its fullness, refamiliarizing himself.

When his lips lowered, he *felt* the beat of her heart, saw the way she gave in to him, even before their lips made contact.

Canton growled low in his throat and grabbed her by her round hips. He moved his hands to cup her soft leather-clad bottom, his hands digging gently into her small but plump globes.

He pried open her mouth and pressed his tongue inside her moist depths. Without pause, her tongue came out to greet his as she brought her hands to rest against his chest, before they eased around his neck, her soft hands tunneling into the hair at the nape of his neck. Dragging him closer.

Canton growled low in his throat. His little vixen was giving him back measure for measure. He thumbed aside her bra that hung halfway off her shoulders, fully exposing her to his roaming hands.

He held her gaze as he leaned down, before capturing one perfect dark wine-colored nipple inside his mouth and sucking.

Her back arched sharply as again, her cry rang out in the room, her hands tightening in his hair.

He released her nipple and watched it spring back to glorious life, plump and filled with blood, beckoning his return.

He laughed a rough, masculine laugh at her whimper of need.

He lifted her into his arms, turned and strolled to the nearest chair, one of the larger ones in the room, one that was built and meant for two to share, never leaving contact with her lips.

He sat down with her nestled in his arms and devoured her mouth with his, his hands swiftly going to work, slipping open buttons, moving the sleeves of her blouse down her arms, along with her bra, and in seconds not only had he stripped her of her blouse and bra, he was impatiently at work on her skirt.

Giving little effort to actually removing it from

her, he shoved the leather up until it was bunched around her waist, leaving her barely there panties as the only deterrent to his lust-filled destination.

With shaky fingers, he ran his hands over her silk-covered mound, his cock so hard, it was a nearly painful thing. But he wanted…needed to taste her. Now.

He maneuvered to gently place her on the large chair before he eased his body to the rug, stationing himself between her legs.

He moved her thighs apart and stared at the object he so desperately needed to taste.

He raised his eyes to meet hers. If she wanted him to stop, this would be her last chance.

"I need you." He could barely choke out those simple words.

Chapter 8

Naomi's body went up in flames.

He gave her no time to think, only to feel. And God, how good he made her feel.

In the recesses of her mind, she knew they had to stop at some point, knew that although she was on birth control, they had no condom available. At least she didn't.

But they'd cross that bridge when they came to it. Now she simply wanted to feel.

And she planned on feeling as much of him as she could.

Her hands had been as busy as his; divesting him of as much clothing as she could, she'd tunneled under his shirt, undoing his buttons as he had done for her. Not with nearly as much finesse and ease as he had performing the task, but with as much enthusiasm.

As she stared down at him, as he knelt larger than life between her thighs, she knew what he was asking her, knew what he wanted to do to her.

His bared chest was thick and ripped with sinewy muscles. Not over the top, but perfectly sculpted pieces of perfection. She hadn't gotten to touch him long enough, and now her fingers ached to run over his chest, to follow the light, furred path that ran down the center, past his rock-hard abdominal muscles and into the sharp V that ended at the top of his jeans.

Jeans she wanted off, to once again feel the perfection of his cock slide deep inside her body.

Even as the thought ran into her mind, she knew she was nearly crazed with want and need for him.

The need she'd had for this man knew no boundaries. Right or wrong, she wanted whatever he would give her.

She bobbed her head up and down, giving him permission to do whatever *he* wanted to do.

At her silent assent, the look he gave her should have scared the hell out of her.

It didn't.

Instead it turned her on to the point she thought she'd embarrass herself and orgasm before he touched her again.

"Good," he roughly bit out.

He leaned down and she held her breath.

He didn't go to the heat of her right away.

Instead his tongue licked the crease where leg and vulva met, the sensitive spot that no man had ever figured out did it for her. But he had long ago. And remembered.

Despite her trepidation, Naomi's body arched against him and a cry of longing strangled her throat; she could feel her pulse beat and stammer a staccato rhythm against his mouth where he'd sucked at the most intimate pulse point on the human body.

As her heart pounded out its crazy disjointed beat within her body, her throat seemed to close in on her. She shut her eyes and inhaled deeply.

Gradually, she calmed and her legs relaxed as he licked around her, sucking and playing with her.

A short sigh of need tumbled from her partially opened lips.

He continued to lick her, playfully, not quite touching her labia, his tongue skirting around the heat of her…lulling her into a sense of calm.

Her eyes had just fluttered closed the moment his lips made the connection to her flesh, his thick fingers parting her as his tongue stabbed deeply into her body.

Eyes now wide and open she moaned, jumping, arching her back away from the chair; she came to a semisitting position and stared down at the blond-haired man between her legs.

The sight of that alone increased the pulsing tension he was creating inside her.

He licked, sucked and tugged on her clit, his tongue sliding in and out of her heat until she felt dizzy with pleasure.

With a helpless little moan, she gave in, her hands grasping his head as he made love to her in the most intimate way.

"Canton… I can't, I mean, you shouldn't…" The protest was breathy and not all that convincing-sounding.

But something in her, something deeply feminine, suddenly grew afraid at how he had made her feel so quickly.

After long moments of lavish strokes from his tongue, he lifted his head and met her gaze.

"You want me to stop?" he asked, his voice low.

A knowing smile lifting the corners of his mouth, his deep voice husky, passion-filled and so erotic-sounding, it did almost as much to her as what his mouth had been doing moments before.

Almost.

With panted breath, she shook her head no. "Don't—don't stop. I mean… I don't know." Real fear was beginning to take the place of the languid sensuality.

She moaned a little in her throat when he gave her a heart-stopping smile with just one side of his lips lifting.

"Give in to me."

The demand was delivered in a velvet voice wrapped in steel. She hesitated before giving him the smallest of nods.

Canton spread her legs again; this time he lifted them so that they lay over each of his big, muscled forearms, before his head went back into the V of her thighs.

His skillful tongue and magic fingers nipped, licked and toyed with her until she thought she'd lose her mind from the pleasure of his touch.

It had been so long since she'd felt anything like what he did for her. Had been so long since she'd felt *his* touch.

Her head fell back on the chair as she did as he instructed and gave in to the mastery of his touch.

With each stroke of his tongue, the flames grew until they nearly engulfed her. When he inserted a finger inside her heat, Naomi gave in to the fiery storm he had created within her.

"Oh, God, oh, God, ohhhhhh!" The last of her cries rose into a high whimper of delight as he used both tongue and fingers to bring her to orgasm.

Naomi's final cry was a wail of pure pleasure, tears of release trickling down her face.

When she opened her eyes, it was to find that Canton had moved to sit beside her, his blue eyes unfathomable as he stared down at her.

He'd put his shirt on but had left the buttons open, and again, just looking at him made her breath catch in her throat.

Yet he said nothing.

God, what had she done? she thought, the stark reality of what had just happened—what she had allowed to happen—sinking in.

Suddenly cold, uncomfortable and embarrassed, Naomi rose from her sitting position and immediately lifted her bottom enough to pull up her panties and yank down her leather skirt, which had been bunched around her waist.

God, she felt like a class A tart, she thought, avoiding Canton's glance, wondering at his silence.

"Here," he finally said, "let me help you." With those words she turned and faced him.

Her eyes fell to his hands, where both her bra and silk blouse dangled from his big fingers. With a mumbled thank-you, she went to take both from him.

Canton pushed her hands aside and did what he wanted—helping her, by turning her back to him and assisting her with her bra.

With a gulp, she accepted his aid, glad for the time, if only brief, to gather her composure. She placed her arms through the shirt and with her back still to him, with shaky fingers buttoned her blouse.

She sat still in that position for a minute, not sure what to say, what to do.

"If I recall right, you said you'd be willing to do

anything to help your family. Did you mean that, or were you playing a game with me?" Canton asked, his deep voice rough with some hidden emotion, one she could hear, but had no clue what it was, what he was feeling.

He turned her around to him, his face still inscrutable. "Like you've done before? Is it all a game for you, Naomi?" Canton ran a thick finger down the line of her jaw, touching the corner of her mouth. Naomi bit back a whimper of need.

Until the entirety of his question hit her...he'd all but said she'd screw him in order to save her family.

"You ass!" she bit out, jaw tightening as she fought away the tears, the amazing way he'd just made her feel, the selfless way he'd taken care of her needs, pushed to the side in her mind.

She shoved his finger away from her face and jumped up from the chair, his callous words too much to bear as raw as she felt at that moment.

Exposed. Vulnerable. Stupid.

All three words perfectly summed up her feelings.

God, what had possessed her to allow him to—She closed down the thought. She turned away from him, unable to look at his face, looking for her purse so she could get the hell out of there before she lost it completely.

"If that's what you think of me, there's nothing more for me to say. I love my family, but I won't prostitute myself for anyone! I'll—" she began, only to have him spin her around and cover her mouth with his hungry lips.

She refused to give in to him. Refused to soften her mouth against the assault of his hungry lips, no matter how badly she *wanted* to surrender.

His kiss softened, coaxing her to submit to his demand.

His tongue snaked out to lap across the seam of hers, before he gave nibbling kisses with gentle teeth to her lower lip, delivering soft flicks with his tongue and biting nips in an intoxicating kiss that had her melting in his arms.

As she had worn low heels, her breasts were on level with his stomach. When his big, muscular arms wrapped tighter around her, it forced her breasts to press tightly against his rock-hard abs.

On and on he licked and bit her, even as his hand stole inside her waist of her skirt, easing inside and rubbing her booty.

As he caressed her, she moaned, her mouth opened and she invited him in.

That was the only invitation he needed.

Eventually he broke the kiss, both of their breaths coming out in harsh, low sounds of near breathlessness.

Canton rested his forehead against hers, bringing her closer, if possible, to his large frame.

"I'm sorry," he said, his voice so low that she barely heard his apology. "I shouldn't have said that."

Simple. Succinct.

Yet his voice was humbly sincere.

Naomi nodded her head, accepting his simple apology. But he wasn't done.

"You do something to me that no other woman ever has. Sometimes, it makes me act like an ass."

His admission, along with the helpless way he ran his hands through his hair, suddenly looking like a little boy, dragged a surprised gulp of laughter from her and he laughed shortly along with her.

He pushed her away. "Besides, this is only the beginning of our...relationship," he said. His head descended, his mouth covering hers again.

His lethal kiss washed away any doubts as to whether or not it was the best idea to enter into a... She didn't know exactly what it was he was suggesting. Sexual relationship? Escort for two weeks? What in the world did he want? she wondered.

Better yet, what was it *she* wanted?

When he ended the kiss, she was unsteady but knew she had to set the record straight.

"But let's get something straight. Whether or not we become...intimate," she began, and ignored the derisive look he gave her, "has nothing to do with the agreement to help my family, correct?" she both asked and demanded. "Because if that's what you have in mind, the answer is no. I will escort you to whatever functions you want, but that is where this 'agreement' ends."

"And if I say no?" he replied, challenging her.

"Then I walk. Point-blank and a period."

He gave her a considering look, his face hardening.

Naomi kept her face void of emotion and quelled the bundle of nerves she felt.

"It's a deal. You come when I need you—according to the deal," he qualified, his face tightening. "And in exchange for that, if you hold up your end of the bargain, my family will help yours out of their... predicament. Does my word work for you or do you need it in writing?" he asked, the tic in his jaw the only indication of his feelings.

She considered the hand he held out. Despite everything, the uncertainty, their tumultuous past and what could become an even more tumultuous present, she knew his word was good.

She allowed him to take her hand, sealing their deal.

He dragged her to him, murmuring, "After what we just did, I prefer a more...intimate way to seal this particular deal," he replied roughly, and took her mouth with his. Before his head descended, Naomi wondered if she had in fact just made a deal with the devil.

Chapter 9

"This time, nothing is going to stop us from finishing what we started. Are you ready, baby?"

Naomi's heart slammed against her rib cage, her breathing coming out in short hitching breaths.

She opened her mouth, ready to speak, to admit what she couldn't, hadn't been able to for over seven years.

"Are you ready for all of me?" he asked, his cornflower-blue eyes staring a hole that seemed to go directly to her soul, reaching in and snatching it out. Her soul, defenseless and of no more use to her, or anyone who was there in his hands.

A garbled sound, a mix of pain and something else, wailed up inside Naomi as she watched him close his fist and crush her soul, her heart...her spirit.

Again, she opened her mouth to speak, to admit a truth she never had before. Not to him, her friends, her mom and dad. Not even to herself.

The sudden insistent *ding* of her alarm finally penetrated her hazy half asleep, half awake state of awareness.

Dare she do it? She'd dreamed of him off and on for years. And now here they were back where they started.

Why had she left all those years ago?

Even to herself, Naomi didn't admit the truth; she'd run from it in the same way that she'd run from him.

But coming back home, lying in the same bed she had seven years ago, as much as she wanted to, she couldn't completely lie or hide the truth. At least not to herself, not anymore.

She'd wanted to feel *everything* with him. She'd wanted to experience everything, not just bits and pieces. As good as those bits and pieces were.

She'd wanted it all.

But not just that. Besides the lovemaking, she'd wanted his love. She didn't know him, had grown up with him in the way that anyone had with anyone else growing up in a community.

They hadn't even been contemporaries in school, as she was a few years younger than him.

But that night seven years ago had sealed her fate.

And scared as hell, not wanting to give up on her dreams, she'd run. And run fast.

And now, seven years later, what was it that she felt, if anything? she wondered, and groaned.

"Nothing. Absolutely nothing. You are not a kid anymore, with a kid's crush. You are a grown woman."

She spoke out loud, softly, ignoring that voice in her head that mocked and scorned her. *A grown woman with a schoolgirl crush…*

Naomi leaned up and grabbed her pillow from beneath her head, before falling back on the mattress, then she smashed it over her face. As though that would smother the very loud, very annoying inner mocking voice, one hell-bent on forcing her to admit a truth she didn't want to challenge.

That realization of truth, one she wasn't ready to address, hovered in her subconscious. To admit the true nature of her fear wasn't something she was ready to confront.

Her eyes were shut tight behind the pillow she still held in place.

Yet a stubborn, single tear ran down her cheek before she slowly removed the down pillow and pulled the quilt her mother had made for her long ago up to her chin and stared up at the ceiling.

"So, baby, how did it go yesterday? I tried to wait up for you, but, well, I must have fallen asleep. Didn't wake up until this morning. With your dad rustling around as loud as he is, who could keep on sleeping?" Roslyn McBride fussed, with a small laugh.

Naomi jumped up in bed and turned, startled and lost in her own thoughts, not expecting to see her mother come through her bedroom door.

With her hand hovering over her breasts in the universal sign of being surprised, Naomi sat further up in the bed, scooting her body until her head hit the wicker headboard. She turned toward her mother's soft voice.

Her mother frowned. "Are you okay, sweetheart?" she asked, concern in her voice, and Naomi smiled, bobbing her head up and down, inviting her mother to come inside her room with a wave of her hand.

Her mother crossed the threshold and walked in, two steaming mugs of what Naomi knew was her favorite cocoa in her hands as she walked toward the bed. She placed the mugs on the side table before she sat on the bed, near Naomi.

A gentle smile graced her mother's lightly aged face as she lifted a hand and pushed away strands of Naomi's curls. Another habit held over from childhood. Naomi's hair was always escaping whatever bun she tried placing it in.

This time it was made messier by all the tossing and turning she'd done last night after returning from her visit with Canton Wilde.

That, and a night of back-to-back dreams featur-

ing Canton Wilde and her, doing things she knew
had to be illegal in a few states.

If not, they should be.

And of course the intimate things she'd allowed
him to do to her…

She felt her cheeks heat. Again, her mother frowned,
and reached out a hand to touch her forehead.

"You're not coming down with anything, are you,
baby?" Her hand moved from Naomi's forehead to
touch her hair softly. "I told you that you shouldn't
have gone outside with your hair wet yesterday!
You'll catch a cold for sure," her mother scolded,
and Naomi laughed softly.

"Mom, first off, my hair wasn't wet yesterday,
but even if it *was*…you can't catch a cold from going
outside with wet hair."

"Well, I know you're the doctor in the family, but
I'm still your mother. And I say stop going outside
with a wet head, girl," Roslyn McBride chided her
only daughter as she lifted the mugs from the side
table and Naomi just nodded.

She accepted the mug her mother gave her and
leaned back against the headboard. "I'm fine, Mom.
Just had a long day yesterday. I had my appointment
with the Wildes," she said, even though she knew her
mother already knew that. In fact, she'd discussed it
with her mother before leaving the day before.

"You didn't tell Daddy, did you?" she asked, reminding her mother of her promise to keep Naomi's involvement in trying to help her parents between them.

"Of course I haven't, Pooh," she said, calling Naomi by the nickname she'd been called since she was a child, which made her almost want to cry.

With all the complications going on in her life, her parents, her career, there were times Naomi wished she could go back to those days of long ago.

"And?" her mother prodded her, gently, concern etched deeply in her dark brown eyes, eyes that were a different shade but as uniquely shaped as Naomi's.

Naomi would do anything she could to permanently remove the sad and stressed-out look from her mother's eyes.

After the deal she made with Canton, she knew she could, yet she hesitated, not wanting to give her false hope, but needing to tell her mother what happened.

"Well," she started, dragging out the word. "I went out to the Wildes' and remember I told you the meeting was supposed to be with Tiber?" she asked, and her mother nodded. "Turns out he's away, overseas on business. So I ended up having my meeting with Canton."

Seeing the optimistic look in her mother's eyes, Naomi was torn. She didn't want to bring her hopes up, but the outrageous bargain Canton had offered her, the ultimatum he'd given her to help her family, was one she had agreed to.

Although she was close with her mother and shared a lot with her, Naomi had never told her about the one-time meeting, up-close-and-personal encounter years ago with Canton.

And there was no way on earth she could ever tell her mother about what she had agreed to with him.

"No matter, sweetie, we'll figure something out," Roslyn McBride said, infusing what Naomi knew was false bravado into her voice. Obviously, her mother thought the meeting hadn't gone well.

"Oh, Momma." Naomi sighed, placing the mug back on the table to wrap her arms around her mother's slight shoulders and hug her. Her mother hugged her back, her hands tightening around her before she gave her a light pat on the back.

Roslyn pushed her away and lightly caressed Naomi's face.

If she didn't know before, if her mind hadn't been made up, looking at the fear her mother was trying to hide from her made the decision a no-brainer.

"Actually, Momma, I have some good news," she began, and forced a bright tone into her voice as she proceeded to fill her mother in.

She left out the intimate details—there was no way she could ever tell her mother any of that—yet managed to tell her of Canton's need for assistance as he attended events in place of his brother. Definitely glossing over all mention of anything of an intimate nature, she led her mother to believe it was simply a business arrangement.

In exchange for her much-needed help, Canton would help the family.

For a moment, while doing the whole *glossing* thing, Naomi felt her face heat with a blush, thinking of Canton and the part she was glossing over.

Naomi thought she saw a look or shadow cross her mother's face, but it was fleeting.

"Are you okay with that, baby? You can take that much time off from going back to work?"

Naomi shrugged. "It's fine, Momma. I spoke with my new boss, Dr. Mason," she replied with a casual shrug. She moved to the side to allow her mother more room on the bed. "I don't officially start at his clinic for a few more weeks. I told him I needed time to spend with the family before I began. He understood. It's not the busy time yet, and the pediatrician I'm replacing is still at the clinic until the first of next month."

"He doesn't know about—"

"No, Mom," Naomi interrupted, her temper rising. "He doesn't know about the family's problems. But really, isn't that the least of *our* problems right now? I mean, is that all that matters to you and Dad? What other people think?" Naomi replied with a sigh.

Pride. Pride was the reason her parents hadn't told her about the back taxes. She brushed aside the irritation.

"You know, Mom, there's no shame in what hap-

pened to you and Dad. If you all had told me earlier, maybe—" She stopped, not wanting to hurt her
mother any more than she already had.

She turned toward her mother, immediately sorry
for her criticism when she saw the hurt look in her
soft dark brown eyes.

Her mother sat near Naomi, stretching her legs
out. She propped her head against the headboard,
mimicking Naomi's posture. Something they had
done from the time she was a child and her mother
would come into her room, and they would talk about
whatever was bothering Naomi.

Work it out. It was what her family always did.
Together. Worked out their problems.

Now, it was her mother and father who needed her
help. She knew at that moment, no matter *what* she
had to do, she *would* do it for her parents.

The two were silent, both lost in their own thoughts.

"Yes, I think it's all going to be fine, Momma.
We'll get through this together," she stated softly,
her mind immediately bringing up the image of the
one man who had never been far from her thoughts,
from the moment she'd returned home.

Naomi placed her head on her mother's shoulder
as her mother stroked her head.

Naomi wasn't sure who she was trying to convince more, her mother or herself.

She forced away the sting of tears that burned the
back of her eyes.

Chapter 10

"Yes, it's coming along as expected. No real bumps in the road to speak of. Hell no, uhh, I mean, no. No, sir." He repeated his statement. "I've got that big oaf covered."

There was a small pause as Cyrus White nervously rubbed the thumb of one hand onto the palm of the other, left eye twitching unconsciously as he did so. He felt his shoulder jerk in symphony.

It was what he did, he knew, whenever he was nervous.

Cyrus knew that his lapse of language etiquette was distasteful to his superior. The twitching got worse. He hoped the man didn't notice it.

He was doing all that he could to move up the chain at Rolling Hills by literally kissing the man's ass. He'd do that if he had to. His superior promised him if he did a good job *this* time, unlike the last job, with that other group of Wildes, he'd bring him in to work directly for him at Rolling Hills.

No more dirty jobs no one wanted to do. He'd be cruising with the big dogs. A grin replaced the twitchy one of moments before.

As he listened to the other man on the end of the line, Cyrus rolled his eyes and whirled his chair around in his seat, staring out over the downtown Cheyenne skyline, doing his best to curb his irritation with his contact and superior at Rolling Hills.

God, get me out of the godforsaken place, he prayed, even though he wouldn't exactly call himself a believer in any deity coming to his rescue. Or a believer in any deity at all.

That ship had sailed long, long ago.

Cyrus White held back a sigh of malcontent as he listened to the boring man continue his even more boring monologue on the importance of patience.

"Patience and due diligence will ensure we win this race," he finished, his haughty voice filled with that irritating superior tone that made Cyrus want to stab the man's eyes out. Repeatedly.

Cyrus's mouth curled in a sneer.

He listened as the man droned on, and on, giving him instruction on how he expected Cyrus to conduct the meet and greet they had planned, in an attempt to finally get the Wildes to come on board.

"You understand this is important."

It was several seconds before Cyrus realized he was expected to answer. He bobbed his head up and down in agreement and wanted to kick his own ass when he realized his nervousness was making him look stupid. He spoke up swiftly, assuring his superior that he did, indeed.

"Very good. Now, surely, I don't need to reiterate to you the importance of getting that 'big oaf' to feel good about what we have planned, no?" he said, and again Cyrus cringed.

Ignoring the pompous way he spoke, along with the fake cosmopolitan accent he'd taken on, one Cyrus knew good and damn well wasn't genuine. Cyrus should know; they'd both grown up in the same poor town in Texas. Despite all that, Cyrus knew his superior didn't miss a thing.

He should have known he'd caught his lowbrow reference to Canton Wilde. He needed to make sure he was more careful in the future.

Like it or not, his superior was his way in, for now at least, to move up the ranks at Rolling Hills. For now.

"Yes, of course. I'll make sure it happens. I'll give him more warm fuzzies than a burlap sack of rabbits in heat."

There was a moment of silence after Cyrus spoke.

Damn it!

As soon as he uttered the crude humor, Cyrus wanted to bite out his own tongue. Would he never learn?

He pressed his fingers to his suddenly throbbing temple.

Would he ever learn the sophistication he needed to impress his superior?

His superior's startled laughter stopped him, mid–mental rant.

For long moments the other man laughed. Unsure if that was a good thing or not, Cyrus nervously laughed along with him.

"Awww, what am I going to do with you, my little friend? You make me laugh, *mon ami*. Awwww," he replied, his surprisingly high-pitched giggle startling Cyrus. "You're going to be just fine!" his superior finished after his laughter had died down.

He was so relieved that he hadn't messed up.... again... Cyrus didn't allow the slur against his height to get to him this time.

Once he'd assured his superior that he had it all under control, he was ready to ask about when he could expect his much-wanted promotion, hoping to at least start the dialogue.

"I've been wondering about what we spoke about the last time, sir," he began, only to realize he was talking to himself.

His superior had already ended the call.

One day…one day he would be the one calling the shots, he promised himself, staring out at the waning sun as it disappeared behind the steel building.

Half the time he thought his superior, whom he'd never actually associated with in person, was never going to do what he promised. Or how many more hoops he'd have to jump through, how many more "jobs," dirty jobs some of them, he'd have to perform to finally get "in."

He wondered. Sometimes he thought his superior was stringing him along, that he didn't have any real faith that Cyrus could get the job done. Didn't think Cyrus had what it took.

Cyrus was always overlooked and underestimated. He knew what to do and how to make it happen. He had orchestrated the oldest Wilde's departure from the scene, and had paid the foreign…scabs, he thought, his lip curling, a lot of money to do so.

He sighed. But it was money well spent. Tiber Wilde thought he was brilliant, that he could outthink Cyrus just because he was a lawyer. Cyrus hated lawyers. They all thought they were smarter than everyone else, just like his superior.

But he had easily manipulated the eldest Wilde. All it had taken was a little money…a lot of money, he mentally calculated, and he'd created an incident the smart-ass lawyer Wilde hadn't been able to get away from dealing with personally.

Which had left Cyrus to deal with the second in command, Canton Wilde.

He could handle *that* Wilde.

A grin stretched his lips wide, revealing perfectly even, symmetrical, capped teeth he'd paid an arm and a leg for...to replace crooked, yellowed ones that had been his legacy from a disenfranchised, poor childhood.

"Now that the smart one is out of the way, it'll be cake dealing with the ex-jock." Cyrus White spoke aloud, his tongue swiping over the perfection of his teeth, his face balled into a derisive sneer.

His fingers steepled together as he stared absently out the window.

True, it hadn't been quite as easy to manipulate the big oaf, as he'd thought it would.

The Cheshire grin slipped.

But he had a plan. All he had to do was convince the Wilde that he could trust him.

Chapter 11

"Yeah, it's all good, Tiber. No real bumps in the road. Nothing I can't handle, at any rate," Canton spoke to his brother via his Bluetooth, while motioning for his assistant to enter into his office. He held out his hand for the small thumb drive Ray, his assistant, held within his hand, one he'd been waiting for him to deliver.

A brisk nod from Canton told Ray that was all that was needed from him, and with a deferential nod, a sarcastic bow and quirk of a brow, all delivered seamlessly and on cue, toward Canton, he spun on a booted heel and left his office.

Subconsciously, Canton registered both the bow and quirk of Ray's subtle sarcasm.

"Ass…" Canton murmured under his breath, noting his best friend/assistant's mannerisms.

"Did you just call me an ass?"

Ray had barely closed the large oak double doors behind him before Canton was inserting the thumb drive into the USB port on his desktop. He absently picked up his rimless reading glasses before he plopped his big frame down in his brother's expensive custom chair. As lavish as the chair was, it creaked as in protest of Canton's one hundred and seventy pounds of pure muscle sitting on its frame.

"Hell, no. Wasn't calling you the ass. That was for Ray," Canton answered, distracted as he waited the less than two seconds it took for the file to open and the info he needed to fill the screen.

"But," he clarified his statement for his brother, "I did call you that earlier today when I met with that even bigger ass, Cyrus White, and had to listen to him go on and on about his company's objection to us buying any more liens. Seemed hell-bent on asking why we felt the need to do that, to continue when the plan was for them to purchase the land that went up for auction. Said a bunch of bullshit about how much better it was for the community, blah blah."

Canton found what he was looking for in the file, his mind split between answering his brother and his task at hand.

"What the fu—" Tiber bit back completing the curse. "That is none of his or Rolling Hills' concern. We will continue as we always have in how we conduct Wilde business." His deep, normally cultured voice was infused with disdain. "In and out of the boardroom, oil field and wherever the hell else Wildes do our business. I trust that you informed him of that fact." Tiber's voice was curt and to the point. And reminded Canton of the way his brother was, once, long ago.

If Canton's attention hadn't been so distracted, he'd call his brother out on his reaction.

"No doubt about it," Canton replied mildly, as a brow rose at his normally calm brother's reaction. "In fact, I told the dumb jerk what he and Rolling Hills could do to the sunny side of my ass. *In fact*—" Canton stopped when his brother interrupted his faux tirade and barked a rusty-sounding laugh.

"Okay. I get the point. I know you can handle any situation, including Cyrus and Rolling Hills, brother."

Canton glanced away from his perusal and sat back in his brother's chair, and frowned.

"Everything good on your end?" he asked, hiding his concern. As the oldest, less than two years separating the brothers, it had always fallen on his and Tiber's shoulders, the well-being of the family on a personal and business level.

Even though the "kids," Brick and Riley, were getting older, not kids anymore, he and Tiber both had a bad habit of trying to do it all—taking care of the business and making sure the family was running efficiently.

"I have faith in Brick. The trip he's on will do him good. He's too damn wild. It'll mature him and make a man out of him," he joked with his brother.

"Like us," Tiber replied, and with a melancholy smile, Canton remembered when both he and Tiber took over the reins of Wilde Oil Enterprises eight years ago.

He laughed, lightly, low. "Yeah, brother. Like it did for us."

For the next several moments the brothers discussed business, until Tiber mentioned a meeting he needed to prepare for the next day.

"Are you sitting in my new chair when I told you not to?"

"Yes. I am in fact breaking your rule and sitting in your pretty little chair. Deal with it." Canton laughed outright.

It was a few seconds before his brother responded as Canton thought he would. He adjusted the volume down on his Bluetooth.

"Take care of the kids." The emotion in his voice again surprised Canton, but he didn't say anything about it. Just let it go.

"Always. You know that." Again, curious at his brother's choice of words and the emotion he clearly heard, Canton frowned.

"Love you, Canton," Tiber said quietly, and before Canton could reply, the phone went dead.

The short delay in communication was another thing he normally held little patience for, as Tiber did. Although they had the best tower for their network, one for Wilde Oil Enterprises alone, the small delay was negligible on a normal day.

On this particular one, it could kick rocks. What the hell was going on with Tiber? he wondered.

He would have continued to try to puzzle it out, but at that moment his door opened and Ray entered.

"Coast clear?"

"Yeah, man, come on in," he replied, his voice distracted. With a shake of his head, he put the subject of his brother on mental ice as he turned back to the monitor.

Ray plopped down on the chair near Canton's desk.

"So what's the verdict? You letting her know what's up? That the Wildes have the tax lien?"

"How the hell did you know about that?" Surprised, Canton's glance flew to Ray. He'd been expecting anything but that to come from his friend's mouth.

"That the Wildes had the lien on the McBride place, or that you haven't told Naomi McBride?" Ray asked and laughed, his voice booming out in the office.

"Both."

"And how long have we been friends?" Ray shrugged a broad shoulder. "Educated guess," Ray continued. "Man, for one, as soon as Dr. McBride rolled back into town, as fine as she is, you'd better believe *every* eligible single man knew within minutes. And you already told me everything about Naomi's situation!" he said, reminding Canton of their earlier conversation.

Then he'd needled him, asking if he minded if someone made a move on her...that was unless Canton had the hots for her...still.

Now, just as he had then, briefly, Canton wanted to knock his good-looking friend's teeth down his throat when he'd mentioned how beautiful she was, and that *he* wanted to make a move on her.

"And two," Ray continued, unaware of or not giving a damn about Canton's irritation, "you forget I was there the night you two...uh, met," Ray finished, examining imaginary dirt under his short nails. Canton would bet his last dollar it was more like his buddy didn't give a crap if he was irritating him or not...in fact, he'd bet his last penny he was doing it *just* to irritate him.

Canton sat back in his chair, saying nothing, just listening.

"You also know her family is in hock. And I'm guessing your plan is to play this out as much as you can and be her knight in shining armor, huh?" Although laugh lines scored his friend's face, there was an undercurrent of…something else besides humor there.

If Canton didn't know any better, he would say his friend was warning him off, as though he would either hurt Naomi or get hurt himself.

"Question is, who you really tryin' to rescue, man?" he asked, his tone casual, but a trace of caution running through his tone.

"Hell, it's not my business either way. So… Ima let that sit right there for a sec. Take your time answering."

The two longtime friends each took the other's measure. What started off as their normal light-hearted banter had turned serious in less time than it had taken for Canton to read the entire file he'd asked Ray to retrieve for him.

For whatever reason, Ray had taken it upon himself, obviously, to look into the file Canton had asked for. So of course he had put a few things together.

Not that he cared. Ray was not only his best friend, but had been his right-hand man for nearly seven years, since he'd asked him to come on board and work with him at Wilde Oil Enterprises.

There were few to no secrets between the two men, and in fact, Ray was like a brother to him.

But even in that, he wasn't ready to play Oprah to his Gayle and open up that damn much. There was only so much "male bonding" a man could do.

"You know so much, inch-high private eye, why

don't you tell me?" he grunted, insulting his friend for the two-inch difference in their height, something he'd been doing since puberty.

As usual, Ray brushed off the insult and laughed. "Naw... I think Ima let you figure that one out, man. Unless you need something else, I'm heading home. And by home, I mean out to find a willing woman who will, as the Staples Singers once sang, 'take me there.'"

"I'm good. I'll catch up with you later," was Canton's reply, his attention back to the file on the screen.

Left alone, he recalled the encounter with Naomi.

It had been two days since he'd left it up to her to contact him next. He knew it had to be her decision ultimately. She had to feel as though she were the one in control.

He'd left a message with her the night she had left him, late, one that had gone directly to her voice mail, as she no doubt had her phone turned off, something he'd wanted. He'd made sure it was late, and in fact didn't want to speak to her. He had been banking on the fact that she'd be asleep and would see he'd left a message the next day.

In the message he'd informed her that if she were willing to take on the "assignment" of being his escort, in exchange for his family trying to help hers to reclaim their land, she had forty-eight hours to decide.

And *only* forty-eight hours.

▼ If offer card is missing write to: Reader Service, P.O. Box 1867, Buffalo, NY 14240-1867 or visit www.ReaderService.com ▼

BUSINESS REPLY MAIL

FIRST-CLASS MAIL   PERMIT NO. 717   BUFFALO, NY

POSTAGE WILL BE PAID BY ADDRESSEE

READER SERVICE
PO BOX 1867
BUFFALO NY 14240-9952

NO POSTAGE
NECESSARY
IF MAILED
IN THE
UNITED STATES

With that, he'd waited. The ball was in her court now. At least seemingly. He knew she'd do anything it took to resolve her family's problems.

The reason for the limited time was mainly due to Canton's impatience to see her again.

He'd tried to lie to himself that it was because he had an upcoming function to attend in less than a week and needed her to come with him if she was on board.

Yes, it was true, he did in fact have a function to attend, one that had he been in the country, Tiber would have attended for the family. True, it was not a Wilde function, but instead one sponsored by Rolling Hills, where some of their top executives would be in attendance.

And the potential deal with Rolling Hills hadn't been inked, and they were still trying to schmooze the Wildes; all of this Canton knew.

He also knew that he would rather be anywhere else but at this party, but because they hadn't made a decision yet, it was his responsibility to represent the family.

If he could, he would have strong-armed Brick into taking his place, but he didn't yet trust his younger brother with a job so important.

Brick still had his Wilde streak in him and hadn't been…tempered…yet, through maturity. In a few years, yes. But now? No, not yet, Canton thought, thinking of his hotheaded younger brother.

Now he was glad he hadn't attempted to strong-arm the youngest male Wilde. If he had, he wouldn't have an excuse to see Naomi and start their deal.

The event wasn't until the weekend, and it was only halfway through the week, so it wasn't exactly an emergency. Canton had yet another plan in mind.

As he'd waited for Naomi to come to the realization she had no choice, a decision he was banking on, he hadn't been idle with his time.

Seven years ago when she'd left, he'd found out as much information about her as he could. He'd told himself it was just out of curiosity.

One of the things he'd learned was that not only had she graduated from undergraduate school early, she'd gotten accepted into one of the most prestigious medical schools in the country, to go into what he later learned was pediatrics.

Upon her return home, she'd secured a position with Dr. Mason, one of the small town's few pediatricians, a man who'd in fact been the pediatrician for him and his siblings growing up.

He'd found it odd that she'd chosen to work in the small rural clinic. With a résumé as impressive as hers—early graduation from undergrad and medical school, internship with one of the leading clinics for neonatal care in the nation—she could have had her choice of clinics to join.

Inevitably, as they had over the past two days, memories of what he'd done to her surfaced in his mind, and on cue, his body stirred to life, remembering how good she'd felt, smelled...and tasted.

It had been hard as hell, pun intended, to put thoughts of her from his mind. The intimacy they'd already experienced, the fact that she had allowed him to do what he had to her, for her, also left little doubt that she was as sexually attracted to him, still, as he was to her.

He allowed his eyes to close, his nostrils flaring as he remembered her scent and her taste. Her smell was as intoxicating now as it had been all those years ago. Her taste beyond anything he'd ever experienced.

His cell rang and he sat up, eyes narrowing in irritation. Until he glanced at the time, a sixth sense telling him who was calling him before he even glanced at his phone. Canton loved Naomi's stubborn spirit.

But he knew that in the end, she'd do the one thing he would have done in the same situation; the needs of the family always outweighed the needs of the individual. He recognized that Dr. Naomi Evangeline McBride would feel that she had no choice but to agree to the deal.

His admiration for her was growing in equal proportion to the hot-as-Hades lust he felt for the curvy pediatrician.

"Fine. I'm in. When is my first...gig?"

The sound of her voice, even through her obvious irritation, was like fine wine, melodic and smooth.

It had been only two days since he'd heard it, and

before that seven years. So why in hell did he miss it as though it had been a lifetime ago since he'd spoken to her?

Irrationally pissed that she enticed him so easily, in a matter of minutes, just like that, with a simple—curt at that—greeting, Canton sought to get back on even footing, his foot being first.

"The event is not until Saturday."

"I thought—"

"I assume you have proper attire. After-five cocktail is fine. And…do you want me to pick you up at your parents' house? I also assume you are staying with them?" He broke into her objections, not wanting to give her the opportunity to steer this particular ship. He had it all under control.

Canton could feel her irritation rise with his purposefully insulting words.

He sat back in masculine satisfaction. Good.

She would follow his lead. Not the other way around. Whether she knew it or not, or liked it when she figured it out or not.

Chapter 12

"Proper attire…"

It had taken her the better part of the day to get up the nerve she needed to call Canton.

Naomi had clamped her mouth shut as his words, all of his words…sank in. She'd opened and shut her mouth so many times she felt like a guppy fresh out of water, desperately trying to figure out the whole breathing thing; she was, momentarily, drowning and out of her depth.

Then she closed her eyes tight, her jaw even tighter, if humanly possible, after the infuriating man drawled the rude question.

As though she wouldn't or *didn't* have the right

attire... She shook off the irritation, reminding herself it wasn't for her, but it was for her folks... She'd reminded herself of that one fact so much over the past few weeks, she could write a hit song about it.

"I think I can rouse something up in the back of the closet, Mr. Wilde, but if you think I might embarrass you, feel free to get someone else to be your date," she bit out, unable to hold back a tiny bit of sarcasm.

His low chuckle should have infuriated her even more.

But damn if it wasn't as sexy as the man who uttered it.

She could see him in her mind's eye, big booted feet no doubt kicked up on his desk, leaning back in his chair as he spoke on the phone with her.

Lord, just give me strength. Not even asking for mega strength, here, God, she continued her prayer. *Just enough that I don't jump through the phone on this man...*

"Are you done talking to yourself?"

"I wasn't—" She stopped, her face flushing with heat. "As I said, I'll do my *best* not to embarrass you," she bit out.

"Good, then we shouldn't have any problems," he drawled, his voice subtly laced with humor.

Naomi again gritted her teeth to prevent herself from saying something she knew she would regret.

Ready to end the call, she was set to do just that when one final question he threw out caught her off guard.

"I think it's a good idea, before Saturday, that the two of us get together."

"And what is the purpose of that?" she asked, wearily. "Besides, I didn't agree to that. I agreed to escort you—"

"I know what you agreed to, Dr. McBride," he began in that irritatingly sexy voice of his, breaking into her objections. "And I also know that you agreed to be at the ready for me when I needed you to."

"I did no such thi—"

"And in order for us to pull off the deception of being a couple—"

"What?! A couple? Look, I never agreed to that! You—"

"—then it's important that you know more about me." He finished as though she hadn't spoken and interrupted him. "So this is, as you see, all a part of the deal. That is, if you want to help your family..." He allowed the sentence to dangle.

Her pause was minimal; thoroughly agitated with the way he was manipulating her, she needed a minute to gather her wits before she went back into battle with him.

She was under no delusions regarding two things with Canton Wilde. One, that he was manipulating the situation and her to his favor. Two, the battle to keep herself in control and not allow him to ever get the best of her was what was in store for her. But there wasn't anything she could do about it, and he knew it. He had her for the next two weeks.

"Fine," she finally agreed. "When and where?"

"Dinner tomorrow night. Six o'clock. I'll pick you up. It's been a while; I look forward to seeing your parents."

"No! I can meet you at—" Naomi's protests fell on deaf ears. Canton had already ended the call.

"Canton!" she yelled out his name as though the sheer volume of her voice would magically force him to stay on the phone.

As soon as she had disconnected, his mocking voice still ringing in her ears, it was all Naomi could do not to hurl her phone across the floor.

But really, who would she be hurting if she did that? She grumbled and not-too-gently put the phone on the coffee table, resisting the urge not to throw it like a major league pitcher would across the room.

Money was tight enough as it was not to do something stupid and destroy her smartphone.

Now relaxing, glass of wine in hand, Naomi sighed and thanked God she was, for the time being at least, home alone. With all that yelling and sheer... agitation Canton brought out in her, she didn't want either one of her parents to know what exactly was going on, not wanting them to worry.

She laughed without humor. Yeah. Worry...if her

parents had a clue what she was doing, or trying to do, to help save the small ranch, their worrying would be the least of *her* worries.

Naomi stood from the couch and made her way through her parents' modest but lovely home.

They'd gone out for the evening at her suggestion. In fact, she'd insisted they do so, both for them, and her, truth be told. She loved her folks, but after being back home she realized that if she were to stay, which she had decided pretty much was a done deal, she would definitely need her own place.

That, and she didn't want them to see Canton Wilde pick her up for their "date."

With a groan, she glanced at the clock and sighed. It was only four o'clock. She had a couple of hours before he would be at her parents' home.

And yes, despite the time, she was drinking a glass of wine. She rationalized that it was five o'clock in Texas and she was still operating mentally in that time zone.

Truth was, she needed everything at her disposal to combat the nerves churning her gut.

These precious moments alone where she could just think had become the highlight of Naomi's evenings for the last few nights. The fact was that she'd been so busy trying to get all of her ducks in a row that by evening, she was completely exhausted. Yet she still had work to do. It seemed the days were too short to complete all the tasks she'd set out for herself.

She and her parents had sat down and had an open and honest talk about the state of their finances. Naomi had confided in them both that the Wildes were going to try to help.

She did not, however, go into detail at all on how she was going to repay them. The Wildes were known to help families in their community out. It was no secret of the wealthy family's philanthropic nature, something their father, Colt Wilde, had been known to do until the day he died.

He'd passed the responsibility of being "thy brother's keeper" on to his children.

She'd fooled around with the truth; although she'd told her mother she would play "escort" to Canton, she hadn't given her any details of what that would entail. Simply saying that she was working with them to get the back taxes paid off, seemed to appease her mother. At least she told herself it had. By "them" she included the entire Wilde clan.

Her parents accepted the half-truth. At least her father had. Her mother had given her the side eye after she had related the story to them, a big fake, over-the-top smile on her face.

She should have known better with the dramatic smile. She went too far with it.

She'd avoided direct eye contact with her mother. She knew her mother was a lot more astute at certain things than her father. And if Roslyn McBride suspected Naomi had a more intimate arrangement going on with Canton Wilde... Naomi suppressed a shudder.

Besides going through her parents' affairs, conferring with them and assuring them that they'd get through their problems, she'd met with Dr. Mason, the elder pediatrician who had run his private clinic for nearly forty years. And showed no signs of leaving.

Instead, she was to be an addition to his small practice, taking the place of another doctor who'd decided to move on.

The quaintness of the clinic was one that appealed to Naomi. The thought of staying in Cheyenne once everything was settled with her parents, and the fear of them not keeping their home was gone, was one that was pleasing to her as well.

Despite the fact that she'd be living in the same community as Canton Wilde, the idea of staying in the small community she grew up in was tempting to Naomi.

Or because of it...again, her inner voice wouldn't let her get away with lying, even to herself.

Naomi debated if she should finish her glass before she had to get ready to face Canton, if for no other reason than to help silence her irritating inner voice.

With a defeated sigh, realizing there wasn't enough

wine in the word to give her the fortitude she needed to face Canton Wilde, Naomi emptied her half-full wineglass into the sink, rinsed out the glass and walked back to her bedroom to get ready.

Chapter 13

The downtown bazaar in Wellsburg was alive and teeming with the hustle and bustle of the early evening.

The early-evening air was crisp; cold enough to require a jacket, but still comfortable enough that Naomi was content walking around without looking for the nearest shop to duck into to warm up.

When Canton had decided they would have their "first date" in the small, touristy town, not far from Cheyenne, she had given him a curious look. It had been years since she'd been there.

"Give it a shot," he'd told her as she settled back into the relaxing leather seat of his truck and turned to stare sightlessly out the window at the darkening sky. "It'll be fun."

Even though he hadn't told her beforehand where he'd planned to take them, rebelliously, Naomi had decided that no matter *what* he had planned she was taking their "date" as casually as she would take him.

With that in mind, she'd dressed in a black denim skirt, tights and knee-high boots, topped with a sweater, and she'd thrown on one of her more casual coats.

Cute, but simple.

A pair of her favorite boho earrings she'd bought from an Etsy store online that reached the top of her shoulder, multiple necklaces and her favorite oversize purse finished the outfit.

She hoped she conveyed the message that being with him, on a date, was not something that called for her to dress up or take any special care with her appearance.

Even though it *had* taken her the full two hours to get ready…and six outfits to go through before she assembled her perfect "I don't care" outfit, she was not trying to impress him.

Not to mention the amount of time it took to pull off her "no makeup" made-up face…or the fact that she'd actually blow-dried her natural curls and flat-ironed her hair earlier in the day…

Nope. She was definitely not even trying to impress him.

She just liked fashion. No more, no less.

His hot gaze had traveled over her head to toe when he'd picked her up, making her flush as he in no way tried to disguise the look of lust in his eyes from her.

Not that she cared, she reminded herself.

In turn, she'd given him the once-over. Like her, Canton was dressed casually in a navy blue sweater, jeans that molded his long legs, and as usual, cowboy boots.

There was nothing special about the outfit, she thought. So why did she have the overwhelming desire to strip him completely naked right there, in her parents' foyer, and damn the date?

Embarrassed at her thoughts, she'd hustled him out of her parents' home, ignoring the knowing look in his bright eyes, as though he knew her lusty contemplations.

"If you're chilly, we can go into one of the shops. A new one opened up I think you'll like, an apothecary of sorts," Canton said, and she turned to face him as they strolled along the cobblestoned streets.

"No, I'm fine. It's been a while since I've been in cooler weather. I loved living in Texas, but I really did miss home," she replied simply.

Naomi had thoroughly enjoyed her time away, but there had been moments, oddly enough, that she had missed the chilly days and four seasons that came with life in Wyoming.

It was good being home.

She found herself feeling jubilant, taking in the atmosphere around them, reflecting on the variety of clientele, from old to young, some wearing business suits, others casually dressed in jeans and sweaters beneath their jackets.

When he'd first suggested they come to bazaar days in one of the smaller neighboring towns, she'd had her reservations.

She hadn't been to the German town in years, and in all honesty wondered exactly why he'd chosen the quaint touristy place.

Those who had grown up in the area were familiar with its history, and although the shops were unique, it wasn't a place she would have chosen for their "get to know each other" date.

But he was captain of this particular voyage, not her.

However, once they'd arrived, memories had assailed her, good ones, of the times she'd come to the town as a teenager, the fun times she'd had there hanging out with friends.

They walked on in companionable silence, enjoying the less-than-frigid evening.

Canton continued to point out shops and entertained her with facts she already knew, and Naomi continued to tease him and remind him that she, too, had grown up in the same area.

"Yeah, yeah… But how long has it been since you've been here, hmm?"

She sighed and shook her head. "Hmm. Okay. It's been a while," she conceded as again, memories of long ago came to mind.

She drew in a breath, remembering… Mingles. That was the name of the bar she'd come to with Alyssa, the same bar where she'd met Canton that night, seven years ago. It was on the outskirts of the small German town.

"Did you ever think of…what happened that night?" The question surprised her so much that she missed a step. Just as she'd been thinking of the night they'd met, truly met, for the first time.

As she stumbled, he caught her under the elbow and helped right her.

Naomi murmured her thanks but stopped walking.

He maneuvered her out of the way of an older couple walking past them, bringing her closer to his body as they stood near the entry to a small bar.

"Was that why you chose Wellsburg for us to come to tonight, Canton?" she asked quietly, her gaze locked with his.

Suddenly chilly, where moments ago she hadn't been, she stuck her hands deep into the pockets of her royal-blue-and-white-plaid coat.

There was a moment where she saw surprise on his face, chagrin maybe…and something more, before he shut his expression down, his face carefully neutral.

"Honestly, not by intention. But I guess a part of me did," he finally answered.

His response was honest, she knew. She glanced away from the intensity of his stare.

"Naomi, did you... Do you miss home?" he asked, his deep voice low. Surprised at his question, she turned to glance up at him, not missing the quiet, contemplative look on his face as he stared down at her.

For a moment, she wondered if that had been the question he'd wanted to ask.

A small gust of wind blew her hair, which she'd left down, across her face.

Naomi turned her head to the side, moving the hair away from her eyes and tucking strands behind one ear, biting her lower lip. She drew in a breath.

The question was innocent-sounding enough and should have been fairly easy to answer. Yet the undercurrents running between them made what should be an easy thing to answer, impossibly hard.

"I don't remember a time I ever saw you after... that night," he said. "It was as though you fell off the planet."

"Sometimes it felt just like that," she replied, the admission torn from her.

She thought of the seven years she'd been away from home. The guilt she felt when her visits to her parents had been shorter and less frequent than they should have been, her fear that she would somehow run into Canton, making the visits home awkward. She'd often opted to stay around the ranch and not go out into town.

That same fear of running into Canton had prevented her from coming home more; had she done that, maybe she would have known of her family's predicament.

The guilt she'd felt because of that fact returned and made her stomach churn.

Ridiculously, she felt the sting of tears burn her eyes.

Oh, God. Please...not that. *Not now,* she begged silently.

"Hey, why don't we go inside? It's getting a little chilly. Don't know if you remember this place, but they have an egg burger that is worth its weight in gold."

Her gaze flew to his.

She didn't know if he discerned her agitated emotional state, or if he were just uncomfortable himself with the turn of the conversation. Whatever his reason for lightening the mood, she was thankful.

With a genuine smile, slight, but real, she nodded her head in agreement, not trusting her voice to speak. When he motioned for her to precede him inside, he placed a big, warm hand at the small of her back, and she allowed him to keep it there as she walked ahead of him.

As she did, she missed the faux smile drop off his sensual mouth, replaced with a look of longing...desire and a lot more.

Chapter 14

"Oh, my, that was good!" Naomi sat back in the cracked leather booth and theatrically groaned.

"*That* good, huh?" Canton asked, chuckling outright at her look of satisfaction.

After the unexpected emotional turmoil he had inadvertently caused her, he'd lightened the mood purposefully. The sadness he saw creep into the depths of her pretty brown eyes was one he didn't understand, yet desperately wanted to go away.

"Yes!" she squealed. "It was *that* good." She licked a finger that held the "special sauce" the bar touted as being the secret to its one-of-a-kind egg burger. Canton bit back a groan at the simple action.

He wanted to lick it, *and* her, completely clean. Head to toe…and not leave a damn thing unlicked, he thought, suppressing a groan.

Something of what he felt must have shown on his face, as her creamy brown skin took on that hue that alerted him that she was blushing.

"So tell me, Naomi, besides the fact that you're back to help your parents, I hear you're joining Mason Pediatrics? Is that true?" he asked, although he knew for a fact it was.

Over the past few days, Canton had made it a point to find out everything his little beauty was up to, including her plans, how long she planned to stay in Wyoming…whether she had a man or not.

She tilted her head in acknowledgment. "It is indeed," she replied, and wiped her mouth delicately, with the cloth napkin.

"How did that all come about? Was that because of your stay here with your folks?"

"Well, two things happened. As you know, the situation with my parents. When I found out what was going on, I started making plans to return immediately. The clinic I was associated with in Texas was closing its doors. So, such as it was, I couldn't have asked for better timing. It made that particular move easier in that I didn't have to worry about who would take my place," she said. "Or who would take over my cases."

As she spoke about her clinic, the children she

served in the disenfranchised area of town, her eyes
lit up. If Canton thought she was beautiful before,
now she simply glowed as she spoke about her life
work. He found himself smiling along with her, encouraging her to share that part of herself with him.

"Actually, my sorority sister told me about what
was going on," she said, shaking her head. "If it
hadn't been for Althea…" She stopped and shrugged
her shoulders. "I have no idea when my parents
would have told me."

A pang of guilt hit Canton; guilt that he could,
with the stroke of a pen, rid her of all worries con-
cerning her parents losing their land. But he couldn't
do that yet. If he did, he'd have nothing to hold over
her.

The selfishness of what he was doing was over-
ridden by his nearly pathological need to have her
with him. For them to finish what they started seven
years ago.

Guilt be damned, he thought.

Suddenly her eyes widened. "And speaking of
Althea. She's married now, to a rancher in Landers
named Nate. Nate Wilde…are you related to anyone
in that area?" she asked and Canton shook his head.

Over the past few years, he and his siblings had
learned of a family of Wildes, all men, and apparently adopted brothers from what they'd gathered.

"Yeah, we've heard about them. More so recently.

Brick was up near Landers on his spring break a few years back and he looked into it."

"And?" she prompted when he fell silent.

"Before Dad passed away, he told us we had family scattered. Not close family; he was an only child. But we think we're related to these Wildes some type of way," he said, his mind not really on the other Wildes. From what his brother told them, these men were brothers, and Wildes, but not by blood.

Thinking of their youngest sibling and the only Wilde woman, Riley, he smiled. She too was adopted, and not Wilde by blood...not that it mattered, as she was just as wild as the rest of them. Sometimes too much.

"What are you smiling about?" she asked, watching him, a small frown of query on her face.

"Just thinking of Riley," he said, and that brought up the subject of his sister after Naomi asked how she was doing.

It wasn't long before the question of his relation to the Landers Wildes came up again.

"I'm just saying, uhh... I think it's a distinct possibility that you all are related some kinda way, don't you? I mean, how many Wilde men can there be?" she asked. There was such a look of incredulousness on her beautiful face at the possibility that there were more Wildes on the planet like him and his siblings that Canton threw back his head and laughed outright at her expression.

Realizing how it must have sounded, she joined in his laughter.

"Baby, I don't know if we are or are not related to them," he said, not realizing he'd called her the endearment. "Really, you'd have to ask Brick. He's the one that has taken to this. A lot lately, ever since he came back from Landers. As soon as he knows, I'll tell you." He paused, his gaze softening as he held hers.

"I'd rather hear more about you and less about any possible distant relatives," he murmured, fascinated and turned on when his statement, for whatever reason, made her blush.

Haltingly at first, she began to answer his barrage of questions. The waiter came and left, refilling their mugs with coffee. Had it been up to Canton, he could have stayed forever, listening to her melodic voice, watching her cute mannerisms as she spoke about the kids and her love for pediatric medicine. Eventually, he feared they'd shut the place down. With a laugh she agreed, and they left the establishment.

Neither one was ready to bring the evening to an end, however.

"Oh, wow, is that what I think it is?" Naomi murmured the question, breaking their companionable silence, making Canton turn his glance away from the light traffic to look at her.

After dinner, they strolled along the streets until the cold had forced them to return to his truck.

After driving for long moments she'd spoken, breaking their silence.

"What?"

With a small nod, she pointed out the back of the window. "Mingles," she replied, and it was then that Canton realized what she was referring to.

A small sign he would have missed, with the name of the club and an arrow pointing which direction to go in order to "get your party on," was off the side of the two-lane highway.

In all of his time coming to Wellsburg, he'd never noticed it. He hadn't returned to the club after she'd left Cheyenne.

"It's still open?" she asked.

"Yeah," he replied, clearing his throat. "Think so. I heard they turned it into a Chinese buffet a few years back, though," he said.

"Seriously?" she asked.

"Seriously, they did. At least that's what I heard." He shrugged. "Like I said, I haven't been there since…you left."

She turned to him; their gazes locked. For a fraction of a moment, time transported them back to that night when they'd first met, and both remembered those initial feelings.

A car honked behind them and Canton turned his attention back to the road.

Again, silence reigned until Naomi cleared her throat and spoke. "Would you mind if…could we drive by there?" she asked, and he heard the hesitancy in her voice.

Not questioning the whys of her request, Canton simply expertly flipped a U-turn and drove down the nearly deserted road that led to what was once a club and now…

"'Mingles Chinese Buffet…and Laundry,'" she supplied, reading the bright neon sign above the former nightclub, unclicking her seat belt so that she could move farther up in the seat and peer through the front window to get a better visual.

The ridiculous of it all had them both laughing hard.

"Oh, my God…you can do your laundry here, too?" she asked, giggling, which set them both off into fresh laughter. This time when their chuckles ended, Canton heard her gasp.

As they'd shared the moment of humor, he realized that she sat very close to him after she'd unbuckled her seat belt. Unconsciously as she'd laughed, she'd moved closer to Canton.

His gaze was focused on her beautiful mouth, the remnants of the smile still lingering on their full lusciousness.

"Uh, I, uh, suppose we'd better get back on the road," she murmured, her eyes on his mouth as well, making no move to go back to her side of the truck.

Before she could, Canton acted.

Moving so quickly, so smoothly that she didn't have a chance to react, much less protest, Canton had the seat moved back into its farthest position, and her straddling his lap.

"I've been wanting to do this all night," he murmured, his hot gaze on her mouth.

Again before she could react, he'd tilted her head, angling her for his kiss.

With a moan she sank into it and him, her legs opening to accommodate the position he'd placed her in, her arms rising so that her hands rested on the back of his head, her fingers immediately tunneling into the hair at the nape of his neck. The times they'd been together, from the first time seven years ago to the most recent time just a few days ago, Canton loved the habit she had of gripping his hair, tugging him closer to her embrace.

Her feminine machismo was a hot thing to a man like him, a man who often had to temper his wilder side; with a woman like Naomi, he didn't.

She gave as good as she got.

Canton made a rough growl deep in the back of his throat, drawing her deeper into his embrace, glad he invested in the auto controls on his custom truck, which gave them even more room to maneuver than a typical truck cab.

She offered no resistance to his silent, rough demand, simply opened her mouth and allowed her legs to further relax...as she gave his tongue entry into her mouth.

He kissed and licked her, biting her full lips, hearing her helpless little mewling kitten-like groans as he teased and sucked the small injury.

As he kissed her, his hands swiftly divested her of her coat, and with her help, he drew it from her body, tossing it carelessly into the backseat.

As soon as his hands were back on her, he brought them back up to shove them under her sweater until he came to her bra.

A few deft movements and her beautiful breasts bounced free.

He broke their kiss, brought her blouse up and lowered his head.

The moment he made contact, brought her nipple deep into his mouth, sucked and tugged on it until it became fat and pulsing in his mouth, she cried out, moaning her delight. Her head rolled to the side as she bit her lip and began to move and gyrate on him, her hands frantically grasping at the back of his head.

In the small, warm confines of his vehicle, her smell was intoxicating. Her scent, her taste, and the way she was moving and grinding on him was all driving Canton insane.

His erection was a painful, stabbing muscle that pulsed and throbbed inside his jeans, yet he gave little thought to his own discomfort.

She was the only thing that mattered.

"God, you smell so good, baby, so good," he mumbled against her mouth, his tongue and lips trailing over her neck, down her collarbone.

She moved her head to the side to give him better access.

"Ohhh, yeah?" she whispered the question, giving vent to her pleasure.

"Yeah," he breathed the words roughly against the softness of her skin. "Like chrysanthemums and lilies on a warm summer day."

Naomi's breath was locked in her throat, as the atmosphere in the truck grew heavy, the air seemed moist and filled with sexual heat. The things he said to her, what he was doing to her, his touch, everything about him turned her on, including the way he smelled.

God, he smelled good!

His aftershave was an expensive one, she could tell, yet not overpowering. It was mixed with his natural odor; the combined scent was unique, heady, enticing and masculine. Just like the man who wore it.

She inhaled deeply.

"You…you smell good, too," she whispered, and blushed.

She was new to the feelings he was generating, new to being this…turned on by a man. She felt inadequate, not sure how to respond.

The only thing she could do, in the end, was to simply give in to the feelings he was generating in her.

"You like this, baby?" he asked, his tone little more than a guttural whisper.

As he licked and kissed her, stabbing her nipples with the flat of his tongue as his other hand massaged the other breast, Naomi was on fire with need.

"Yes, yes," she answered, her own hands as busy as his.

She brought them up beneath his sweater and groaned when she encountered his tightened male nipples.

He growled low when she squeezed one, and she laughed a feminine sound of delight.

"Do you want me to stop?" he asked, his breath on her breast warm as he spoke, and she paused.

She felt his body tremble, yet his hands remained still, waiting for her to give him the okay.

God, she was so needy for him. On fire for his touch.

She could no more say no than she could stop breathing.

"No," she breathed. "Don't stop."

He licked the tip of her breast, making his way down the front of her chest, licking and kissing every sensitive spot and nerve along the way.

Naomi squirmed, caught between his big body and the press of his hands bringing her into tight contact with that part of him she had longed for, dreamed of, for seven years since she'd had him the first time.

When his hands went to the hem of her skirt and

hitched it up, she lifted her bottom to help him. He yanked down her tights until they were completely out of his way.

When her nearly bare ass tapped against the rough denim she moaned, squirming against him, feeling his erection against her bottom.

He stilled her gyrating hips, growling against her mouth a warning, "Careful."

She laughed, breathless, feeling a sense of feminine power at what she could bring out in this man.

"Think that's funny, huh?" he asked.

His arm tightened around her lean waist, and he brought her into close contact with his shaft. Both of his hands moved to her hips and lifted her up just enough so she cleared his lap, only to bring her back down.

Over. And over and over...

"Ohhhhh, Canton, what are you doing?" she moaned, crying as he slowly ground her against him, his tongue fastened on one of her breasts as he worked her up and down on his shaft.

He inserted a hand between them, shifted her wet panties to the side and in one smooth move, inserted a thick finger inside her clenching heat.

"I need to feel your mouth," he said and she opened up to him.

"Canton, if we don't stop, I'm going to——" She stopped, cried out as he jerked her against his hand, working her as though it was his shaft, moving her so that she felt her body tremble, on fire; she knew if he didn't stop, she'd come.

As badly as she wanted it, she wanted him to feel good, too.

He'd given to her before without taking anything for himself.

Although the orgasm had been amazing, there had been a part of Naomi that wasn't fulfilled. She realized it was because she hadn't given him the same pleasure he'd given to her.

But not this time.

As he kissed her, she felt the tautness of his lips, the control he must be exerting that left his big body trembling, all giving testimony to how badly he, too, needed *something*.

She made her decision.

She eased her own hand between them, moved his fingers away from her panties, her heat, enough so that she could feel the heavy bulge pressing into her.

"Baby, no...what are you doing?" he asked, groaning. He broke their kiss and rested his forehead against hers as she stroked him through his jeans.

Not good enough, she swiftly unzipped him and released his shaft, running light caressing fingers over the mushroom head, her fingers coming away wet from his precum.

"Baaaaby, hmmmmm," he moaned, helplessly moving against her hand as she ran her entire hand, top to bottom, over his long, thick cock.

Naomi was so wet, so excited, she knew it wouldn't take long to take her over the edge.

With hesitant moves initially, she caressed him; worried that she wasn't doing it right, she asked, "Is it…is it okay? What I'm doing?" in a near whisper. "Does it feel goo—" Her words were cut off on a long whimper when he readjusted their positions so that as she stroked him, he could go back to pleasuring her.

"Yes, yes…don't stop." He grunted the words against the corner of her mouth.

A lone finger circled and rubbed her clit, spreading her moisture around the tight, blood-filled nub that was so engorged it bordered on pain for Naomi, the pleasure was so intense.

When he plunged her depths with one finger and added a second, she grew dizzy, her breaths shallow. But as good as it felt, the mindless sensation of pleasure mounting to incredible heights, she continued to stroke and caress him.

Her small hand was barely able to form a complete fist around his massive shaft, yet she was reassured with his growls of pleasure.

Canton thrust his fingers deep inside her body as his other hand maintained a grasp on her hips, moving her with him as they rocked against each other.

Soon, she felt the beginnings of her orgasm unfurl deep within her belly.

"Canton… I, oh my God, I can't, oh, I, I—" Her

rambling cries for help against the sensual storm were met with feral growls and stinging kisses until she felt her body give in to the pressure.

She came, long and hard, her body shaking as she allowed the orgasm to consume her. As though from a long distance away, she heard him come, felt his body jerk.

When the heat of his seed erupted, Naomi kept the pressure where he needed it, instinct guiding her, as finally, with one last upward thrust into her palm, he collapsed back against the headrest, bringing her body down, her head to rest on his chest.

She closed her eyes, the strength of her orgasm, the wonderful feelings he'd created, all soothing her mind, body and soul.

After he'd dropped her home with a promise to see her the next day, Naomi felt as though she were on cloud nine; never to her recollection had she ever felt so light. Never could she remember feeling so…right.

All the puzzle pieces of her life fit. If only for this one time, it all fit.

She didn't want to examine the whys of it. She simply wanted to enjoy the feeling for what it was.

As she prepared for bed, a flush heated her entire body as she thought of how he had, again, first wanted to take care of her needs and not his own. Just as he had before.

Not that she'd allowed that to happen again, she

thought, blushing. She'd been afraid she didn't know what in the world she was doing, having never done that to, for or with a man before. But his groans of pleasure and the way he'd released...yeah, she figured she'd done it right.

A giggle bubbled out of her mouth and she shook her head at herself. He had her acting like a schoolgirl, she thought.

She threw on her pj's and climbed into bed. For the first time in a long time, she found herself drowsy quickly, and before she could marvel at that, she was asleep, an expression of contentment on her face.

Chapter 15

"Canton, do you remember when you asked me about my parents, and whether I missed Cheyenne or not? You know…about the town, and everything?"

Canton placed the last book on the shelf from the large stack she'd placed in front of him, with the instructions to "put these in order."

Naomi was placing what appeared to be the last of her stack on the shelf near her desk, next to her computer. After she placed the large tome onto the smaller shelf she examined her work. With a nod of satisfaction, she turned and walked toward him.

He watched in amusement as she tilted her head, left and right, then went about rearranging a few books until with a satisfied grunt she declared, "All done!"

Impatient to feel her against him, he tugged her to his body. "You were saying?" he asked, reminding her of her question.

Or the beginning of one.

Canton moved her body away so that he could see her face better.

"I remember my question…" he gently prodded her, tucking the always-there errant curl back behind her ear.

He'd learned that at times, despite being a brilliant woman, Naomi could lose track of where she was in a sentence, or the fact that she had even asked a question. Or been asked a question.

Or needed to answer a question.

Pretty much if she were involved with anything to do with medicine, even her office and how to arrange her things to her satisfaction, there was a strong likelihood that she would become absentminded.

Rather than being a turnoff, it appealed to him. She was brilliant. A little scatterbrained at times, but brilliant nonetheless.

They were in her office after meeting downtown for lunch. She'd shyly invited him to come back to her clinic if he was interested.

He'd quickly assured her he was. He was greedy for her. In the time they'd spent together, Canton had quickly wanted to know and learn as much about her as he could, greedy for knowledge about her, thirsty to see the sight of her beautiful face, starving for a taste of her lips…her body.

But he'd bided his time.

He wanted, scratch that, needed for her to come to realize that what was between them was strong. Needed her to come to trust him and ultimately want him as desperately as he wanted and needed her.

When thoughts of the lie of omission he'd created weighed heavy on his mind, he forced them away. He knew soon enough he would tell her the truth. He had no other choice.

Not only because it was the right thing to do, but because he would catch the worry that would occasionally show up in her beautiful brown eyes. Canton knew that thoughts of her family's situation were never far from her mind.

But the time wasn't right. He would tell her soon, once he felt secure enough in her feelings for him. Feelings he knew were growing deeper as the days went by.

The week had flown by; each day, as he'd promised her, they spent in communication. Whether it was lunch or a phone call, there hadn't been a day that had gone by that he hadn't spent time getting to know her. Allowing her into his world and letting her get to know him.

The "shindig" as she laughingly called it was set for the weekend and a part of him wished he'd lied…

and told her there were more events to attend. But he was hoping by then that he could be up front with her about everything, including the lie of omission he'd led her to believe that he would "help" her family in exchange for her assistance.

"Oh. Yeah, right," she said, laughing softly and shaking her head at her own lack of memory.

When her face lost a bit of its animation, he frowned. Yet he waited for her to speak.

"Well, remember when you asked me if I…missed the town?" she continued and he again nodded his head.

"Yeah, I remember, babe…why?"

"I did. I mean…miss the town, that is," she replied softly.

Canton frowned and tilted his head. When she ducked her head as though to avoid his gaze, he placed two fingers beneath her chin and brought her face up, forcing her to meet his gaze.

"And?" he prompted, drawing out the word.

"And, well, that's all. I missed the town. Umm. A lot. I thought about the town a lot, too."

He frowned, not understanding why she felt the need to tell him that.

"Okay, well, that was expected, baby. But I'm sure you were busy, school, establishing yourself in your field." He knew she was going somewhere with this, but didn't know exactly where.

"Canton!" she said, and balled a small fist up

and gently tapped him on his chest. The fact that he barely felt her strike him seemed to make her even more agitated.

She struck him again. This time he caught her fist, brought it to his mouth and opened her palm.

He placed a kiss in the center, keeping his gaze on hers the entire time.

"Kisses, not hits," he said softly, as though he were talking to a child, much the same way she would to one of her young patients, fighting to keep the smile from his face.

"Butthead," she said and laughed. "That wasn't the only thing I missed."

He felt a smile tug the corner of his mouth. Was his recalcitrant woman trying to tell him something?

She drew in a deep breath, and as though it was the hardest thing to do, then looked him in the eyes. She literally squared her shoulders.

Canton didn't know if he should be happy...or concerned. He hoped it was the former and prayed to God it wasn't something he didn't want to hear.

The last few weeks they'd begun to build a rapport so strong, he wondered if she realized how easy she had become with him, how much she had begun to open up to him.

"I missed you. When I left that night seven years ago, a part of me left...because I was afraid."

The admission wasn't what he'd expected to hear.

Canton put all joking aside and sat down in her

desk chair, pulling her down with him, stealing her protest with a short, hot kiss.

"Continue," he said, once he'd released her mouth.

She drew in a deep breath and began. "My folks are hardworking people. Although my mom went to college, she didn't finish; she met my father before she did, they got married…and well, to the day, nine months later I was born," she began with a small laugh.

Canton listened to her as she opened up about her family, not wanting to speak in case she lost her nerve and stopped. He silently encouraged her to continue.

"The night I met you, it seemed like everything changed for me. I had known of you, your family," she said. "I mean, who didn't know about the Wildes? But that was unlike anything that had ever happened to me. The way we seemed to connect from the first…well, it scared me. And after we made love, well…"

As her voice trailed off, Canton didn't press it. That night had seemed just as magical to him as it had to her. He didn't know how or if he should share with her just how much it and she had meant to him.

He allowed her to continue.

"The next morning, when I woke up…in, um, the hotel, well, I felt cheap. I knew your rep." She laughed without humor. "Everyone did. And to be honest with you, I thought I was just a onetime deal with you. That it would be easier for you, and me, if I was gone before you woke up. So I left. A part of me wanted you to come charging after me," she went on, shaking her head. "But...well, when you didn't, I figured I was right and you weren't interested. I graduated a couple weeks later and left for medical school."

Canton remembered the anger he felt when he realized that not only had she left, she hadn't even said goodbye to him. In his youthful, righteous anger, he let her go. Thought she'd come back.

By the time he realized she wasn't, she was no longer in Cheyenne.

For long moments she sat in his lap, listening to his heart as it beat steadily against her ear, remembering that time long ago.

She didn't know what had come over her, but the closer they'd become, the more she wanted— needed—him to know how much he'd affected her that night. Why she'd left and never returned.

"So, why did you leave?" He got to the heart of the matter with the simple question.

"Fear." The answer was as bold as it was concise. She sighed. He wrapped his arms around her and she leaned into his embrace.

"Fear that what I felt wasn't real. Fear that if it was real, you didn't feel the same."

He placed his chin on the top of her head as the memories flooded both of them.

"You know, I felt the same way."

She leaned her head back far enough to look up into his handsome face.

"I had never felt the way I did that night. It was like there was no one in the world but the two of us. From the moment I laid eyes on you to the moment we fell asleep in each other's arms. I knew it was different. I guess I was a little scared, too," he said, the admission surprising her anew.

"You? Why?"

"Tiber and I had the responsibility of the family on our shoulders with Dad's death," he began and she nodded. She, like everyone in the community, was saddened by the death of the Wilde patriarch, although everyone knew of his love for smoking his favorite cigars; he'd been diagnosed with cancer and months later it had spread throughout his body.

"With that, not only did we have the company to manage, we had Brick and Riley as well. And those two..." He allowed the sentence to dangle and she giggled lightly, as she'd heard the antics of the two youngest Wildes growing up, as well as from Canton the past few weeks.

She felt his pride as he spoke of his siblings. "That and a few personal things had happened that threw me, baby. To be honest with you, I was still sorting through some issues that rocked my world, even as Tiber and I had to hold it together for the family."

"So…had I stuck around, then what?" she asked after a long pause.

He shrugged and lifted her chin, forcing her to look into his eyes. He gazed down at her. "Oh, who knows…maybe nine months later we would have been welcoming a little Wilde of our own into the world."

His reply brought a swift hiss of what was a combination of pain and desire for what might have been from Naomi.

He knew she was using the incident of her parents as a factor on their own situation, but the thought of seeing a little brown baby with his bright blue eyes staring at them was so real, so…vivid.

For a moment, the words seemed to affect Canton. A flare of emotion shone big and bright in his eyes. To recognize the truth of his emotions. Even though neither one of them had yet said those three important words to each other.

"So…what do we do now?" she asked in a low voice.

He stroked a hand over her curls, and she lay closer against his chest.

"We keep doing what we're doing now." He surprised himself with his answer, not for what he said but the wealth of emotions that lay beyond the words.

Chapter 16

"Well...how do I look?" Naomi performed a perfect pirouette for her parents, holding the ends of her gown out with both hands, one leg extended, posing for full effect.

"Aww, look at my baby girl. You look stunning, sweetheart!"

As soon as she came into the living area, both of her parents were there, as she knew they would be, sitting on the sofa together, talking and watching television nonchalantly.

But Naomi knew the real deal; they were not only waiting for her to come out so they could ooh and aah over her, but also they were waiting for Canton to arrive and pick her up for the evening event. Particularly her father, she knew.

Naomi was the slightest bit nervous about her dad's meeting Canton. She was nervous for two distinct reasons, each reason associated with each man.

For Canton, she had no clue how he would act around her father, what he would say. She doubted he would mention their arrangement, no way on earth! In fact, she had all but forgotten their agreement. She was confident he felt the same.

No, she was worried for a whole different reason. Ever since the day she'd gone to his job, their relationship seemed to have grown. Although it had only been less than a week, she felt the changes. The nuances small, but easy for her to see and feel.

Which was the other reason she was nervous about Canton coming. Although they'd been inseparable as much as possible, being in the other's company from the moment she'd come back to town, Canton had yet to really come into contact with or formally be introduced to her parents.

He'd come by one day to surprise her and take her out on one of the Wilde oil rigs. The drive was long, so her mother had packed them a snack. Embarrassed the slightest bit, she'd opened her mouth to tell her mother they were fine. And promptly shut it when Canton greedily rubbed his hands together like a villain in a cheesy action film and thanked her.

With a laugh, his mother had smiled, hugely, the

light lines that scored her mouth only making her prettier.

Just like that, Canton had gotten her blessing.

Her mother had given him her approval silently, winking at Naomi as she walked out the door with him, hand in hand. When she mouthed "Ooh, yes, ma'am!" Naomi tried to quell her giggle. Whenever her mother liked something or someone…anything really, her standard reply was a drawn out, "Ooh, yes, ma'am!"

Her father had been out on his land working and had missed Canton's visit. But Naomi doubted Canton would get his approval so easily. Not only because she was his only child, but she worried that her father would be embarrassed because of their financial situation.

She hadn't really discussed anything further with her parents, only assured them that all was going to be okay.

For the first time in a long time, she believed that herself.

"Baby, you look absolutely beautiful." Her father spoke and she turned toward him; her big grin faltered at the look in his light gray eyes.

Because she had her mother's dark-toned complexion, most people would automatically say she favored her mother, but in actuality, it was her father Naomi resembled more.

One of things she'd definitely inherited from her

father was the way he'd frown and bite on his bottom lip when he was either lost in thought or worrying.

Right now he was biting on his lip so hard, she thought he'd chew it off.

He turned to her mother. "Baby, would you mind getting me a refill on my drink? I want to talk to Ne Ne," he said, and her mother nodded her head and placed a hand over Dean McBride's lightly tanned brown hand and squeezed.

"Of course, darling. In fact, if it can wait a second, I think I left something in the bedroom. I'm going to grab it real quick." He nodded, and with a wink she left Naomi and her father alone.

"Dad?" she asked, her frown mirroring his. He smiled and held out a hand to his daughter for her to take.

"Baby, come and sit down for a minute. I need to tell you something. Something that's long overdue," he began and a ball of anxiety pitted her stomach.

"It's not all that bad. Get that nauseous look off your face, baby girl," he replied gruffly, kissing her cheek as she sat down near him on the sofa.

"What is it, Daddy?" she asked, staring into her father's light gray eyes. Despite his assurance, worry and fear were beginning to make her sick.

"It's about the money. Where it went, and why we couldn't pay our taxes," he began. "Your mother and I started saving up for your college the minute you were born. We never told you that, because, well, by the time we needed the money to send you to school, we had already used it."

She frowned, not saying a word, just listening to her father's heavy words.

"Well, to be honest we didn't use it for ourselves, or you. We used it to help the Carsons," he said, mentioning a family she'd grown up with in their community. "Around the time a lot of folks were losing their shirts, we were still holding on. Some of our friends weren't so lucky. The Carsons were one of them. Well, they lost the lien on their house to that company, the one that's been sneaking around buying up the land 'round here. That Rolling Hills," he said, spitting the name out.

Naomi wasn't surprised at anything her father was telling her. He went on to say that he'd lent money to the family to try to pay back the tax lien, but it hadn't been enough in the end.

Not only had the Carsons lost their small ranch, they'd lost all of their money, along with the money the McBrides had lent them, and were unable to pay it back in time for Naomi to go to college.

"Daddy, I don't understand. How did you and Momma pay for my school, then?" Confused light brown eyes met saddened gray eyes. Without a word she understood; it was all there for her to see.

Her parents hadn't been able to afford to send her to school, and despite the scholarships, there had been a large amount they needed to pay. Medical school wasn't cheap. But she hadn't known. Although they never discussed it with her, she'd always assumed they had a college fund for her.

"We got out a loan. The next year, and a few years after that, well, the money got leaner, and we missed a few payments on the taxes. And, well..." He allowed his sentence to dangle, but there was no need for him to say anything more. Naomi easily filled in the rest.

"Oh, Daddy...why didn't you tell me?" she asked and reached out her arms to hug her father, love and understanding making tears burn her eyes.

The sacrifices her parents made for her, the love they shared, was something she would always cherish.

"It's all going to be okay, Dad, wait and see. We got this," she said.

"Yeah, we got this, baby girl," he replied. She laughed through the burn of tears when he offered his closed hand for a fist bump.

She grabbed him and hugged him, pouring all the love she had for her father into her tight embrace.

When Canton arrived at her parents' home to pick her up, she proudly introduced her father to him.

She could barely keep her eyes off her man; he was so fine, so resplendent in his tux, she felt everything feminine in her leap, jump and tingle at the sight of him.

His tux fit him as though it had been custom-made.

Actually, she realized it was. Tall and broad-shouldered, he was the epitome of what a man should look like wearing a tuxedo. The expensive fabric fell perfectly on his lean, muscular form; the nontraditional black shirt he wore beneath it was a perfect foil against his light-colored hair and eyes.

She noted her mother's smile and blushed, caught staring at Canton as though he was the last drumstick at a Thanksgiving meal.

And just as expected, each man sized up the other; Canton because he knew the love the small family held for one another was strong. He knew that if Dean McBride didn't think he was worthy of his only child's love, he'd have a hell of a time taking their relationship to the next level.

As far as Naomi's father, he scrutinized Canton, grilled him on what his family was doing, how they were helping the community, and barely, just barely, refrained from asking what Naomi knew was burning a hole in his tongue to ask.

The same question all of their neighbors wanted to know…what were the Wildes' plans with Rolling Hills?

The fact that he refrained from asking point-blank was a relief to Naomi. Finally the two left and he escorted her to his vehicle. Expecting the truck, she was surprised to see the low-slung, late-model silver Jaguar in her parents' driveway.

Naomi knew her parents were watching them from the window of the den.

She knew Canton was just as aware of their regard.

He opened the door for her. Before he helped her into the low vehicle, he turned her into his arms.

"God, woman, could you be any more beautiful? You are the beginning to my end," he told her, a catch in his voice as his gaze roamed her face. She gasped at the incredible words, a wealth of emotion springing forth, catching her off guard.

Before she could think of a suitable retort, he kissed her as though he would never see her again. The kiss was a statement to her parents.

She felt it, knew exactly what statement her Wilde man was giving.

When he released her, she tried as hard as she could to keep the smile from her face. To no avail.

"Are you ready to knock 'em dead, baby?" he asked, chuckling when she could only mutely nod her head up and down, still reeling from the romantic words he had spoken to her moments before.

The moment they entered the ballroom at the Grand Hyatt, the place where the cocktail party was being held, Naomi felt nauseous.

It wasn't the grandness of the event or that she felt as though she didn't belong. Instead, it was the man who'd rushed to greet them as soon as they'd entered: Cyrus White.

Immediately he'd begun fawning over Canton, barely listening as he introduced Naomi, in such a rush to "speak to my Wilde man."

Naomi barely, just barely, suppressed a shudder.

She frowned at his choice of words, caught Canton's glance and saw his reaction as well. Good. It wasn't just her. Cyrus White was definitely acting too familiar with Canton.

She placed a faux smile on her face and when Canton grabbed her hand, placing it within his big warm clasp, and winked down at her, all of Naomi's irritation vanished as though it never were. The connection with him was so real. Just like her family, she felt deep down in her soul that he had her back.

She grinned up at him and giggled a little when her wink made him stumble. He leaned down, brushed his mouth against the side of her ear—sending goose bumps over her skin in the process—and threatened her.

"If you insist on teasing me, be warned, you'll give me no choice but to find a dark corner somewhere and show you what happens when big girls wanna act like little girls...and tease big boys."

This time it was her turn to stumble just the slightest bit, at both the hot warning and the subtle swat on her backside he gave her. He gave her a concerned, angelic smile and helped her stay steady on her feet, asking if she was okay for those listening, the look in his bright blue eyes anything but saintly.

Chapter 17

Naomi moaned into his mouth and drew in a sharp gasp when he shoved her gown down her shoulders, slipping it down farther until it pooled at her ankles, revealing her tiny panties and lacy bra before his hot gaze.

They had barely made it inside his house before they were all over each other.

Naomi had never been so glad for a keyless entry system than she was that night. It allowed him to open the door with a remote device even as he rolled into his own private entry to the Wilde mansion.

He swiftly, expertly parked his car in the attached garage, which also would lead them directly to his own private living quarters, something each of his siblings had in the Wilde mansion as well.

Grabbing and kissing each other, Naomi wanted him just as naked as he wanted her, and just as quickly.

She was so impatient to feel him, to lose herself in his embrace, that she nearly tore the pearl buttons off what had to be a very, *very* expensive tux.

Before she could stop him—had she wanted to—he'd released her mouth and trailed a line down her body with his tongue, leaving a fiery, scorching wet path in his wake.

He was crouched down low in front of her.

He lifted one foot and then the other from the confines of her dress and she stood over him wearing nothing but her underwear and stilettos.

He kept his eyes trained on hers as one big hand came out to cover her mound beneath the silk of her bikini panties.

His long, thick forefinger feathered back and forth over the front of the silk, and she nearly came from the look in his bright blue eyes; the clarity of his intent was obvious even before he acted out the wicked promise within them.

"I've been wanting to taste you all night."

His words were hot, direct, and Naomi groaned when she felt the heat of his mouth over the silk of her panties.

* * *

Canton had never been so damn hot for a woman as he now was with Naomi.

Neither had he ever felt the kind of love for a woman that he did for her. He'd known it the first moment he laid eyes on her. He hadn't told her yet, but he planned on making up for that, and more.

Thinking of the small box inside his dresser drawer brought a growl of possession. She was his.

After tonight, he planned on telling her everything…and then proposing.

But now, he planned on making love to her properly. Seal the deal so there were no more questions about who she belonged to.

He leaned into her, inhaling her unique intoxicating feminine scent, burying his entire face in her heat. He could probably smell her like this and come, she was so damn intoxicating to him.

The entire night, he'd been unable to concentrate on anything or anyone but her.

A part of him knew his focus should be on the task at hand, that he should have been interacting with the Rolling Hills crew with more attentiveness; he and his brothers had to make a decision regarding Rolling Hills soon.

If nothing else, he'd learned tonight that his instincts were right; there was definitely something wrong with Cyrus White more than ever. The little man left a sour taste in his mouth.

But that was something he'd have to discuss with Tiber as soon as he brother returned home. For now, his mind, his attention, his everything was only on the woman in front of him.

He thumbed her panties aside, hearing but ignoring her sweet little gasp as his gaze centered on her pretty feminine spot.

Canton leaned in and licked her across the seam, leaving the silk damp.

"Canton," she groaned, bucking against him. "Come on!" she moaned, laughing breathlessly.

"That's exactly what I plan on making you do…" he replied, laughing low, rough, a masculine sound of appreciation when her knees buckled and again she called out his name.

He would have allowed her to join him on the floor and eat her out right there…but he wanted to feel her buck against him as he loved her in this position.

"Baby, I want to feel all of you, experience all, not just—" Her moan echoed off the walls and he grinned against her mons.

He separated the lips of her vagina. "You will. Eventually," he promised, before licking her between her hot, wet folds.

"What are you doing to me, baby?" she moaned, her hands reaching out to grasp his head; not to push him away, but to hold him steady, right where his baby wanted him to be, as he licked, stroked and loved her, intimately giving her what she needed, what she wanted and deserved.

He loved her so much he ached with desire. He could spend a lifetime on his knees giving his woman pleasure if that's what she wanted.

He took his time with her, licking her, fingering and caressing her until she grew so weak her knees would no longer support her standing.

He allowed her to fall to the floor, following her, his big body hovering between her legs. He lifted them, placed them over his arms and leaned back into her.

Canton took the end of his tongue and laved her tight little bud over and over until he knew she was seconds from exploding.

Then stopped.

"Nooooo!" she groaned, head tossing on the soft rug, and he suckled her, his pursed lips against the hub of her core.

"I'm going to take care of you, baby. I'll always take care of you. You believe me, you trust me, don't you?"

Naomi was robbed of speech; never before had she been to this level, this height of arousal.

When she nodded her assent, again he catered to her, licking her, stroking into her heat, until she felt like a bomb ready to explode. She begged him. Pleaded with him to let her come this time.

She nearly wept with pleasure when he appeared

to give her what she so desperately needed. As he licked and stroked her, he added a finger inside her clenching core, thrusting it in and out, preparing her for his shaft, knowing he wouldn't be able to last long, that he needed to be balls-deep inside her.

This would be their first time in a long time having full penetration. He remembered how small she was seven years ago, how he'd had to prepare her. As he pumped his fingers in and out of her, his hooded gaze watching as she writhed on the floor beneath him, he felt his cock harden to granite, as he realized that although seven years had passed, she was still hot, wet…and tight.

Just when he knew she was about to release, he shifted and moved over her. With deft precision, he removed the condom he'd hastily grabbed and sheathed his erection. In one long, hot glide, he impaled her with his cock.

She screamed the minute he slid all the way in, but he didn't stop. Beyond his rational mind, Canton lost control.

It had been so damn long since he'd felt her, so long since he'd felt a fraction of what he felt for her with any other woman. The pleasure was so intense, it was nearly blinding.

He groaned when he felt her hands, hesitant at first before they grew bolder, grip the edge of his cheeks, digging into them, before one hand slid down and cupped his balls.

Canton stiffened when her nails scored his back at the same time she played with his testicles.

He knew she was innocent. Just as innocent as the day he'd first met her, but the way she was playing him, she was giving him more pleasure than women with ten times her knowledge ever had.

Sweat poured from him, landing on the hollow of her tummy as he stroked inside her heat.

"How do you—" He couldn't complete the question. At that moment she squeezed, lightly, on his sac and he felt his orgasm swallow his questions.

He gave in to it, but he wasn't going alone.

He grabbed her hips, brought her up to meet his thrusts and slammed into her hot, welcoming heat with a ferociousness that would not be denied. He spread her legs as far apart as they could go, and leveled one leg up to get at a better angle to feed her more of his cock.

"Oh, baby, it's good...sooo good," she cried, weeping with the strength of her emotions, accepting, welcoming the power of his trusts.

When she met his thrusts one final time, he exploded, detonated, on the spot. His orgasm swept her up along with him as he came and came and came... coming for so long and so hard, he felt weak, but full. Depleted but powerful as he held on to the woman he loved more than he thought possible to ever love.

As she milked the last of his seed and he was nearly spent, he yelled, "I love you, Naomi!"

With a cry of acceptance, she wrapped her arms around his neck and gave in to her own release.

"Yes! I love you, Canton, I love you I love you I love *youuuu*." The litany rolled off her tongue as waves of pleasure and release crashed into them, leaving them both weak and completely satisfied.

After their bodies had cooled, he lifted her from the floor and carried his beautiful burden with him on to the bed.

Naomi woke to feel Canton's big, hard body spooning her, her bottom lying close to his shaft… as he played with her.

She moaned, releasing a long sigh, opening her legs to give his talented fingers better access.

"I could wake up like this for the rest of my life."

At his words, her hands stilled on top of his, which lay on her belly. Seconds later she went back to her light, feathery strokes.

She didn't know if she'd ever felt this relaxed, this good in her life.

To say Canton was an extraordinary lover was putting it mildly. What he did to her body, how he made her feel both in and out of bed, was something she'd never felt before.

For a moment, fear and anxiety filled her mind. He'd said he loved her, but had that been in the heat of the moment? Could he really love her a fraction of the amount she loved him? she wondered.

When he lifted her bottom, and slowly, so slowly she felt every hot inch of him glide into her body, all thoughts and insecurities vanished. For now, this was what she wanted. What she craved.

Languidly, his strokes even, slow, he made love to her. Naomi reached an arm back and up, bringing his mouth close to hers; she kissed him, the position allowing only the corners of their mouths to touch, the tips of their tongues to meet and play as he stroked into her heat.

Unlike their first, more frantic coupling, there was a difference this time. Her body was still on fire for his, and she knew from the rock-hard sensation of his cock and the tight feel of his sac tapping against her seam that Canton felt the same. But this time, they were able to slow the pace, as though by mutual agreement. They were able to draw out their lovemaking…marinate in it.

"Hmm," she moaned when he pressed the palm of his hand on top of her mons and pushed.

"You like that?" he asked, and she could only nod her head.

"Good," he replied with a harsh laugh. "Because I want to make you feel good, just like this, for the rest of your life."

Again, he alluded to them being something more, and Naomi allowed her eyes to close and imagined…

His strokes continued, becoming more demand-ing, more urgent. Soon, she felt her belly tighten in the pleasure/painful way it did when she was on the precipice of release.

She squeezed her legs together around his cock, keeping the tether tight, and her movements began to match his, growing in excitement she bucked against him, and within moments he'd given her what she needed.

This time Canton came at the same time as Naomi; his thrusts strong, hard, sure he leveled into her giving her all that he could, all that he had within him. His love for her, as his seed, bursting from him as he came, giving her what he'd never given an-other woman; allowing her to claim him as he was claiming her.

When Naomi woke, it was to find Canton next to her, with his big, beautiful, naked and *incredibly* sexy body sprawled out, a contented look on his face.

As hot as he was, as much as she loved him... Naomi knew she couldn't handle another round. Not until she'd had a long, long soak, she thought.

She smiled softly, thinking of how many times they'd made love and how many times he'd told her he loved her.

Her life had never been so complete.

Not only did she have the man of her dreams, but she also would be helping her parents. One thing she was sure of if nothing else after being around Cyrus White, the man would do anything to win Canton's approval and to get the Wildes on board with Rolling Hills.

She doubted they'd overly protest the Wildes' bailing her parents out. With her help, her family would pay the Wildes back. She loved him, and knew that part was going to be tricky, his being okay with the repayment.

She smiled down at his sexy sleeping form.

But she'd find ways to make sure he was okay with it.

Gingerly, not wanting to wake him, she eased from the bed. A quick trip into his adjoining bathroom to use the facilities and she was washing her hands. Glancing at the mirror, she grimaced, placing a hand to her rat's nest of a hairdo. She quickly finger-combed her curly tresses and with efficiency from years of practice pulled the mass of hair into one single braid, the ends landing with a thud in the middle of her back.

"Well, that's about as good as it's going to get," she said.

Quietly she walked around, glancing at Canton only to see he was still knocked out. With a little grin, realizing she'd put that man to sleep, she tiptoed out and left the room.

She'd been to his home more than once, and allowed instinct to guide her to the kitchen, hoping she wouldn't meet anyone on the way there. Lucky for her, no one was.

She opened the beautiful oversize refrigerator. Had she not been in his kitchen before and not known it, she might have mistaken the refrigerator for a cabinet, as its doors matched those of the equally gorgeous redwood paneling on the floor-to-ceiling cabinets throughout the kitchen.

Naomi was in the process of grabbing the orange juice when a small *ding* caught her attention.

Frowning, she spun around, trying to locate the sound until she realized it was a phone and shrugged.

Now she needed a glass…hmm, she thought. Which cabinet would she find one in?

She was so thirsty she was very tempted to chug it straight from the bottle when a deep, masculine voice, one eerily similar to Canton's, spoke. Naomi jumped and nearly dropped the container of fresh juice all over the perfectly clean granite counter.

It dawned on her that first, some unseen answering system had picked up the call, and second, it was Canton's older brother, Tiber, on the other end. She didn't know people even used answering machines anymore. Curious, unashamedly she listened to his brother speak, a smile on her face. Wow, the two brothers sounded alike. But she knew the difference right away. Her Canton's drawl was the slightest bit more…earthy than his brother's.

Way sexier.

Hmm.

She shook her head at herself. She had it bad, no lie about that. Somewhat listening but not really, Tiber's next words stopped her cold.

"Lastly, I got the report on the liens. Good to see you're taking care of the McBrides. Out of all of the liens, it's good to know Rolling Hills didn't have theirs. I agree with you, it's in our best interest to have it. Okay, so answer your damn cell phone, would you? I feel like a fool calling a landline. Who the hell does that anymore?" his brother griped. Had Naomi not been in a state of shock, she would have laughed that he'd somewhat echoed her sentiments.

With that the static on the other end he'd disconnected the phone.

She let the entire conversation soak in.

He had deceived her.

From the beginning he'd hidden the truth.

Rolling Hills didn't have the lien to her family's land. The Wildes did.

Tears ran unchecked down Naomi's face.

Gaining momentum, the scalding tears fell down onto the counter as, numb, Naomi couldn't move a muscle.

It was then she heard a sound. She glanced up to see Canton in the doorway, frozen, his handsome face staring into hers.

Her face hardened, turning to stone.

"Wait, baby, I can explain!"

"Save it. God, I was so damn stupid! To think you actually cared about me." She threw the angry words at him, but immediately stopped and shook her head.

"It's not like that, and you know I do! If I didn't, I would have let your family suffer from your father's inability to take care of his household, but I didn't!"

She turned stricken eyes toward him, his callous-sounding words putting the final nail in the coffin.

"Damn! Baby, I didn't mean it like that, please!" She ran away him, darting around his big—naked—body; she evaded his outstretched hands and ran into the bedroom.

She had to get away. Now.

Canton watched Naomi gather her clothes. He went to touch her and she drew back as though he'd struck her.

"Leave me the hell alone!" she bit out; her anger a tangible thing, her hand whipped out and slapped him, hard, across the face.

Before he could react, before he could run after her, she'd left.

After the shock of her slap had worn off, he hopped one foot and then the other through the legs of his tuxedo pants from the night before and tore through the house. By the time he made it to his garage, the door was opening and his woman and his Jag were nothing but a cloud of dust.

Damn it!

Chapter 18

Canton had completed no less than ten drive-bys, circling the entire area where Naomi's family resided, along with three other small ranches. Finally, before he got arrested, he came to a halt and parked his truck in front of her family's home.

Although it was cold, he cut the engine, not wanting to draw her or her family's attention before he was ready.

If any of her neighbors caught him driving by at ten miles an hour, as secluded as the area was, they'd have the CPD on him in two point two, as Naomi would say.

Thinking of Naomi and her funny little sayings

brought the beginnings of a smile to tug at his lips. God, he missed her like hell.

Canton sighed, thinking of the last time he'd seen her.

It had been two weeks. The first day, he'd come by her house and had been told by her parents that she was not home and was out with a friend.

Struck with a jealousy so wild, so out of control, his first thought had been that the new doctor who'd joined the clinic was the one his woman was out with.

So pissed off, he'd lost it, demanded to know who she was with, with his face tight and fists balled at his sides, anger rolling off him in waves.

It was then he learned where Naomi had inherited her dual nature. She could be as sweet and mild as any man could want. Pliant, loving and the best lover he'd ever had.

But then…well, she could go into beast mode. He'd witnessed the swiftness with which she could go from lamb to lion when prodded.

He'd always thought of Dean McBride as mild-mannered, a very easy-tempered man.

Until it came to his daughter.

In no uncertain terms, he'd told Canton, his gray eyes now cold, that he knew what he'd done, how he had manipulated his child.

His face, a much lighter brown than his Naomi's, was flushed with anger. He'd gone on to tell him that he would pay his family back every cent of the "blood money" they owed. Plus interest.

"I don't know if my daughter told you the whole story, Mr. Wilde. Why we got into trouble financially in the first place."

Hesitatingly, Canton shook his head no. The older man, with pride in his voice, told him the story of how and why his family had gotten into debt. Canton noticed that as Dean McBride spoke, he didn't try to make himself out to be a hero, either for paying Naomi's way through school—in Dean's words, that was his responsibility as a father and provider—or for helping his neighbor in times of financial hardship. Again, that was what he believed his job was to do.

Much as the Wildes believed they were their brother's keeper.

There were others, much less financially well-off than the Wildes, who felt the same spirit of community.

Canton was humbled.

After he finished speaking, the pride in the older man's eyes light gray eyes as he met Canton's gaze made Canton feel like an idiot. And a jerk.

He also realized how much he loved Naomi. She held the same sense of self as her father, the same love for family and community as well. He thought back over everything he'd learned about her, from the first moment he met her until now.

God, he loved her.

The kind of deep, soul-wrenching love that a man was lucky to come across once in a lifetime.

"I'm sorry, Mr. McBride. Please, please forgive me. It was never my intent to hurt her." Even to his own ears, he heard the desolation in his voice. Though simple, his words held a wealth of emotion.

Dean McBride's eyes had warmed and he'd invited Canton inside his home. There, the two men had discussed the terms of the repayment of his debt to the Wildes.

Canton never had any intention on asking for any repayment, but knew Dean's pride would never allow that.

After that, he'd told Canton that he and his wife planned to go out of town for a few days.

Canton hadn't understood why he told him that until he went on further to say they would ask Naomi to come and take care of the cat and plants for their two-day "staycation," as Dean referred to his and Roslyn's trip to a neighboring town.

A genuine smile graced Colton's face.

He was going to get his baby back.

In his demand to try to find out who she was with, instead he'd learned yet another thing about the woman he loved: she came from a family as devoted to one another as the Wildes were.

He'd called her cell to no avail. He had eventually given up when it would go directly to voice mail. Either she had a new phone or a new number, or whenever he would call, she'd decline it. Either way, she wasn't answering him.

He'd gone by the clinic as a last resort, and had been gently but sternly turned away by Mrs. Mason.

But he had Dean McBride on his side. He'd opened up to the man and told him how much he loved his daughter. He'd see her. Soon.

Now, as he sat in his truck, the engine cut, he still hesitated.

She was inside, this much he knew.

Her father would only help so much. He wouldn't give him a clue to how his daughter was feeling. But that was fine with Canton. He was a man and knew how to get his woman. He'd apologize for being an ass and not telling her up front that his family had already bought the lien, which would have saved her the stress he'd been able to relieve.

And she would forgive him, and they'd live happily ever after, damn it.

He shook his head at his own machismo. "Okay, so why are you still sitting in your truck, then?" he chided himself.

Damn. He hadn't realized just how much he loved her until he'd hurled the careless words at her.

The hurt look in her pretty brown eyes had haunted him for the past two weeks.

He ran a hand through his disheveled hair.

She was so far under his skin, he felt her even when

she was nowhere around him. The love he had for her had been building from day one, seven years ago.

He jumped out of his truck and slammed the door behind him.

But not before he checked the pockets of his jacket to make sure he still had the little square box he'd been carrying around for the past two weeks.

It was now or never.

With purpose in his stride, he walked toward her front door.

Chapter 19

"Hold on, hold on!" Naomi mumbled as she stumbled off the sofa, the pounding on the door finally penetrating the fog of sleep.

She righted herself and squinted, glancing over at the corner of the room and the grandfather clock.

Who in the world would be coming here at this time of night? she wondered, noting the near midnight hour.

Her parents weren't supposed to be back for a few days.

But even so, they would hardly need to knock to gain entrance into their own home.

She stood, pulling the white wifebeater she wore of Canton's down to cover her, even though the shirt fanned nearly to her knees.

As she neared the door, right before she rose on tiptoe to peep through the little window, a feeling swept over her, an awareness...

Canton Wilde stood on the other side of the door. Her heart jackhammered against her rib cage.

Emotional tears burned the back of her eyes, but she refused to give in to them. She'd cried enough over the past two weeks.

He had his head bowed, hands buried inside his leather bomber jacket.

She glanced down at herself, but didn't have time to run and grab a robe. With a mental shrug and a large sigh, she unlocked the door and opened it wide.

"Hey."

His deep voice resonated through her body and Naomi's glance rose to meet Canton's as he stepped inside the foyer, closing the heavy door behind him.

"Hey..." she replied, a catch in her voice

Once she got a good look at him, a soft cry escaped her lips.

A rough stubble covered his lean cheeks; his hair was disheveled; lines of fatigue scored the sides of his sensual mouth.

"God, I missed you," he said before she could speak. Reaching out, he roughly pulled her to his body, enveloping her in his warm embrace.

Naomi bit back the cry of love she felt wanting to tumble out of her mouth.

She didn't know what to say, didn't know what

she should say. She knew only that she missed him so much, she'd felt empty without him.

But she was still so damn hurt by him.

When she made no response, simply allowed him to hug her, he finally released her, setting her back from him.

He stared at her, nostrils flaring, waiting, she knew, for some response from her...

A small tic in the corner of his sexy, chiseled mouth was the only indicator of how he felt; his blue-eyed gaze, steady, unflinchingly locked with hers.

She broke her glance with him and ran her eyes over him, head to toe. In addition to his hair being disheveled and obviously in need of a trim, the stubble on his face was heavier than what it appeared to be from initial observation.

"I trusted you."

When she finally spoke, she saw the immediate response from him to her words. Emotion flared to life in the depths of his bright blue eyes quickly before dying out.

He opened his mouth to speak, but she beat him to it.

"Not only did I trust you, I believed you were a good man. I even felt guilty about leaving that night." She felt a burn in the back of her throat and stopped, her eyes clogged with tears.

"But obviously I made the right decision. I thought you were nothing more than a careless playboy who didn't really give a crap about anyone besides himself and his precious Wildes, and I was right." She bit out the words and turned away before he could read the emotion she knew was in her eyes.

"My family is all I have. Just like you. We're proud, yeah, okay, I'll give you that. You were right about that. But there was more to it than that. Mom and Dad worked hard, damn hard, to put me through school. I had no idea until recently how hard," she began and felt the threat of tears fall as she thought again of her parents' sacrifice for her.

As much as she loved him, remembering the nasty words he threw at her made her want to slap his chiseled mouth.

She began to back toward the living room, not really caring if he followed her or not.

At least, that's what she told herself.

For a moment she thought he wouldn't. She'd nearly made it to the living room when she heard the sound of his boots hitting the wood floor, and seconds later, before she realized his intent, big hands grabbed her, turned her around and hauled her into his arms.

"Canton, let go of—" Her words were swallowed in his mouth, her body in his embrace.

Lifting her high into his arms, he made love to her mouth as he walked farther inside her parents' home.

Finally he released her mouth enough to mumble around it, "Which way?"

"Huh?" she asked, dazed and confused, her hands grasping the back of his head, as she gave in to the demand of his kiss.

"Bedroom. Yours."

The succinct way he spoke, the harshness of his voice, all told her what she already knew; Canton was holding on by a thread.

"Straight back, last door on left."

She didn't even try to fight him.

What was the use, anyway?

He found his way to her bedroom in the semi-dark house. If she'd been in another frame of mind, she would have ribbed him on how easy it was for him to find it.

But not now.

He reached her room, but didn't bother flipping on lights as he went directly to the bed and dumped her on the soft mattress.

Canton followed her down, never losing contact with her lips. In between muffled kisses, groans and moans, they frantically began to undress each other, each anxious to get at the other.

She knew they still needed to discuss some "stuff." But not now.

"Baby, I missed you so damn much," he said, framing her face within his big palms. "I don't know how long the first time will last…" he said and she groaned with the feel of his big, naked body covering hers.

"Baby...it's okay. I'm in the same boat," she said, and he laughed shortly.

He slipped a hand between their entwined bodies, separating the lips of her vulva and testing her readiness.

She moaned, burying her head in the crook of his neck, embarrassed at how wet she already was for him, and he'd barely touched her.

He growled, bringing his finger to his mouth. Forcing her to watch, he licked her cream completely from his finger.

"Baby...love me," she begged. "Just love me."

That was all of the encouragement that Canton needed to hear.

He tried his best to be as gentle as possible. But it had been so long since he'd felt her wrapped around him. And he was so damn hard, so randy, he was lucky he didn't embarrass the hell out of himself and spill outside her, before he got the chance to feel her.

"Damn it!" he growled, and her frantic eyes met his.

"*What?!* What is it?" she asked, her body grinding against his, searching for what she needed, what he wanted, to bring them both the release they so desperately craved.

"No condom."

There was only a heartbeat of silence. Then his baby brought her small hands between them, reached down, grasped his cock and guided him to her entry.

"Baby...? You sure?" he asked, a wealth of emotion in his voice. He knew, more than words, what it meant for her to silently accept him with no protection.

With a groan, he helped her guide the pulsing head into her welcoming body, as he carefully, as gently as he could, pushed inside until he was seated fully inside her body, his balls hitting the lips of her vulva.

Once embedded, Canton stopped, forehead meeting hers, not moving; he savored the feeling of being back inside this amazing woman.

He felt complete.

He'd *never* had such a feeling of wholeness, of... rightness, as he did now, inside Naomi.

He adjusted her onto his shaft and, grasping her round, sexy hips, began to rock slowly inside her.

As badly as he wanted to go balls to the wall with her, give her *all* of him, fill her up until she flowed over...with him...he tried his best to keep it slow, relaxed as he nestled inside her warm heat and rocked inside her.

He needed to come, needed to feel her come around him, but still, he took his time with her.

As he made love to her, as they made love to each other, he wanted to savor it and her.

Relish and marinate in her.

Drown himself in all that was Naomi.

They'd been together a short time, all things considered. Yet it felt like a lifetime.

He wanted to give her a lifetime of loving and wanted to receive the same in return.

Naomi knew what he was doing, knew he wanted to go slow with her. But she wasn't having it.

And she knew just what to do to get her man to give her what she wanted.

She buried her face in his chest. Her tongue struck out, licked his male nipple as she wrapped her legs around his lean waist, her heels digging into his firm, tight ass.

"Goodness, baby…what…what are you doing to me?" he asked, his voice harsh, breaking.

She could feel how close to the edge he was, knew that if she weren't careful, he'd go completely over. That along with his rough talk turned her on even more.

"I missed you… God, I missed you," she replied, her own voice little more than a whisper as she met his long, languid strokes as he glided in and out of her.

He was feeding her just enough, enough to get her feeling good, right, but not enough to take her over the edge.

He picked up the pace and lifted one of her breasts. His tongue snaked out, stroked the nipple, before his mouth engulfed the upper swell. Naomi's body hummed and tingled, the beginning of her orgasm hovering.

"Canton…oh God, oh God, oh God…" She began

the low chant, her fingers tightening in his hair at his nape, as she began to give in to the feeling he was helping to create inside her.

As his thrusts picked up cadence, so did his attention to her breasts, first one and then the other. With his sucking and strokes, she was losing her mind in the sensation of feeling.

She reached between their bodies and cupped his tightly drawn sac, gently caressed it and smiled a feminine grin when he growled against her breasts in obvious pleasure at her touch.

He released her breasts, threw his head back and yelled as he released.

"I love you, baby, I love you, Naomi!" he yelled as his hot seed jettisoned into her body.

"Yes! I love you too, Canton!" Within seconds, Naomi was joining him.

As she accepted his seed, accepted him, their screams of release and passion echoed and rebounded off the bedroom walls as they reached satisfaction in unison.

Chapter 20

"Do you love me enough to stay with me and never leave me again?"

At his hoarsely asked question, Naomi would have shot straight up in bed, had she the energy to do so.

As it was, she could only move startled eyes to where he was now propped up next to her.

She ran loving eyes over him, her hand reaching up to cover and cup his shadowed cheek.

"I think we need to talk about a few things first, don't you?" she asked, tugging on her lower lip, her eyes darting over his beloved face.

She loved him. She also knew that he loved her. But...

"I know. I was an ass. I'm sorry, baby," he began, and she leaned back on the pillow, keeping her gaze on his.

"Go on..." she encouraged, fighting back the need to smile from pure happiness.

Canton saw her struggle to keep from smiling, and his heart did that crazy flip it did whenever she smiled at him. Hell, whenever she was within a forty-mile radius of him.

He was worried she would never forgive him for hurting her so badly. After making love to her, some of his worries had been alleviated. Some. But not all.

He knew he had to give her everything. No holding back.

While she'd been recovering from their lovemaking, he'd reached down and grabbed the square box inside his pocket. He kept it behind him, knowing that he needed to speak from his heart first before they could move forward.

He took her hand in his and brought the box from behind him to hold loosely in the other.

"Naomi McBride, you invaded my heart, my mind and my dreams seven years ago."

He saw her inhale a deep breath, her eyes darting from his to the box he held in his hand.

"But, first things first," he said, dreading her reaction. "About your family's lien. I know I should have told you from the beginning that we held it.

But, to be honest, baby, I didn't know how." He ran a hand through his hair, in frustration. "You didn't trust Rolling Hills, and you damn sure didn't trust me. If I told you we had the lien, I was afraid you'd run away from me. Again." He locked gazes with her. "And I wasn't going to let that happen again."

"Baby, it's okay… I understand." Before Naomi could finish, Canton leaned toward her, and kissed her softly, lovingly. Slowly he released her

"No matter how many times I told myself it was just a one-night stand, that it was meaningless, I never forgot you. When you came back into my life, it wasn't a coincidence. It was meant to be. I fell in love with you the moment I met you and the feelings haven't faded; they only have grown." He tugged her closer to him and gave her a kiss on her open mouth.

He released her and opened the small box.

The perfectly gorgeous princess-cut royal blue sapphire, her favorite gemstone and one of the colors of her sorority, was surrounded by diamonds, and it nearly blinded her.

She smiled through the tears.

"There is nothing I don't love about you, Naomi."

He lifted her hand, and she watched as he brought it to his lips.

She allowed him to slide the ring onto her finger. It fit perfectly. In that moment she knew that just like the ring, the two of them fit together, with as much perfection as the ring on her finger.

The tears now trickled down her cheeks. Naomi felt no need to try to stem their flow.

"I don't want to go back to dreaming of you, as I did for seven years. The question is, do you love me enough to see past my faults and love me as deeply as I love you?"

She bobbed her head up and down, smiling through the tears. Joy welled up within her. The last two weeks without him in her life had been hell.

She, too, remembered what it was like to think of him, dream of him...and not be with him.

Naomi had, from the time she was a child, prided herself on her ability to communicate.

But now, words failed her.

She stared into the cornflower-blue eyes of a man whom she knew, without doubt, she loved more than anything in the world.

But as she wrapped her arms around him and nodded her head against the strong column of his throat, she heard his loud "hell yeah!" and laughed around her tears.

He pulled her back, his eyes filled with love, and captured her mouth. The toe-curling kiss was over too soon, but she allowed him to lift her and straddle her over his big body as he plopped back on the bed.

Naomi's last rational thought before he filled her was his sheer...*wildeness*, telling her that it would indeed be a riotous ride at times, living and loving a Wilde.

But it was one wild journey she was looking forward to experiencing, for the rest of her life.

* * * * *

From their first kiss…

IT'S ONLY You

SHERYL LISTER

Record label VP Donovan Wright saves ER nurse Simona Andrews's life, and she promptly declares she won't date him. Donovan is a media darling, and since she became her niece's guardian, Simona wants to avoid high-profile affairs. Yet Donovan's touch sets her on fire. Before she walks away for good, he has one chance to prove that his promise to love her will never be broken…

Available September 2015!

KPSL4190915

REQUEST YOUR FREE BOOKS!

2 FREE NOVELS
PLUS 2 FREE GIFTS!

KIMANI™
ROMANCE

Love's ultimate destination!

This summer is going to be hot, hot, hot
with a new miniseries
from fan-favorite authors!

YAHRAH ST. JOHN
LISA MARIE PERRY
PAMELA YAYE

HEAT WAVE
OF DESIRE

HOT SUMMER
NIGHTS

HEAT OF
PASSION

Available June 2015 *Available July 2015* *Available August 2015*

California Desert Dreams

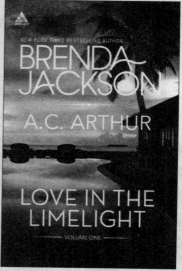

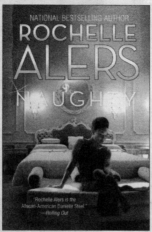

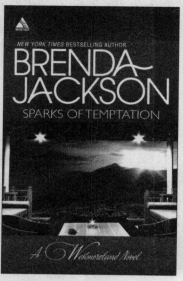